Sports Illustrated KIDS
GRAPHIC NOVELS

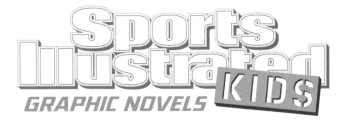

STONE ARCH BOOKS
a capstone imprint

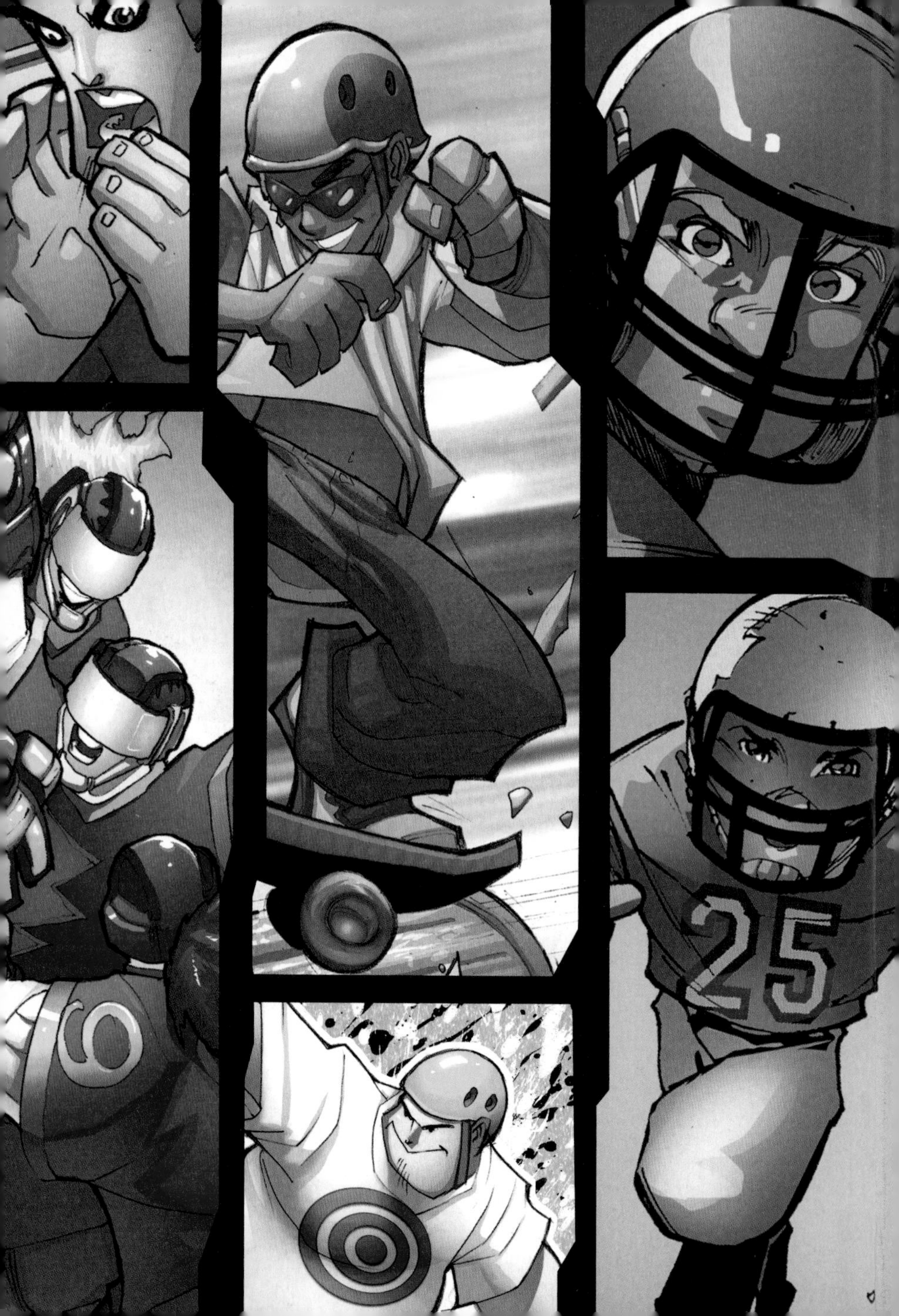

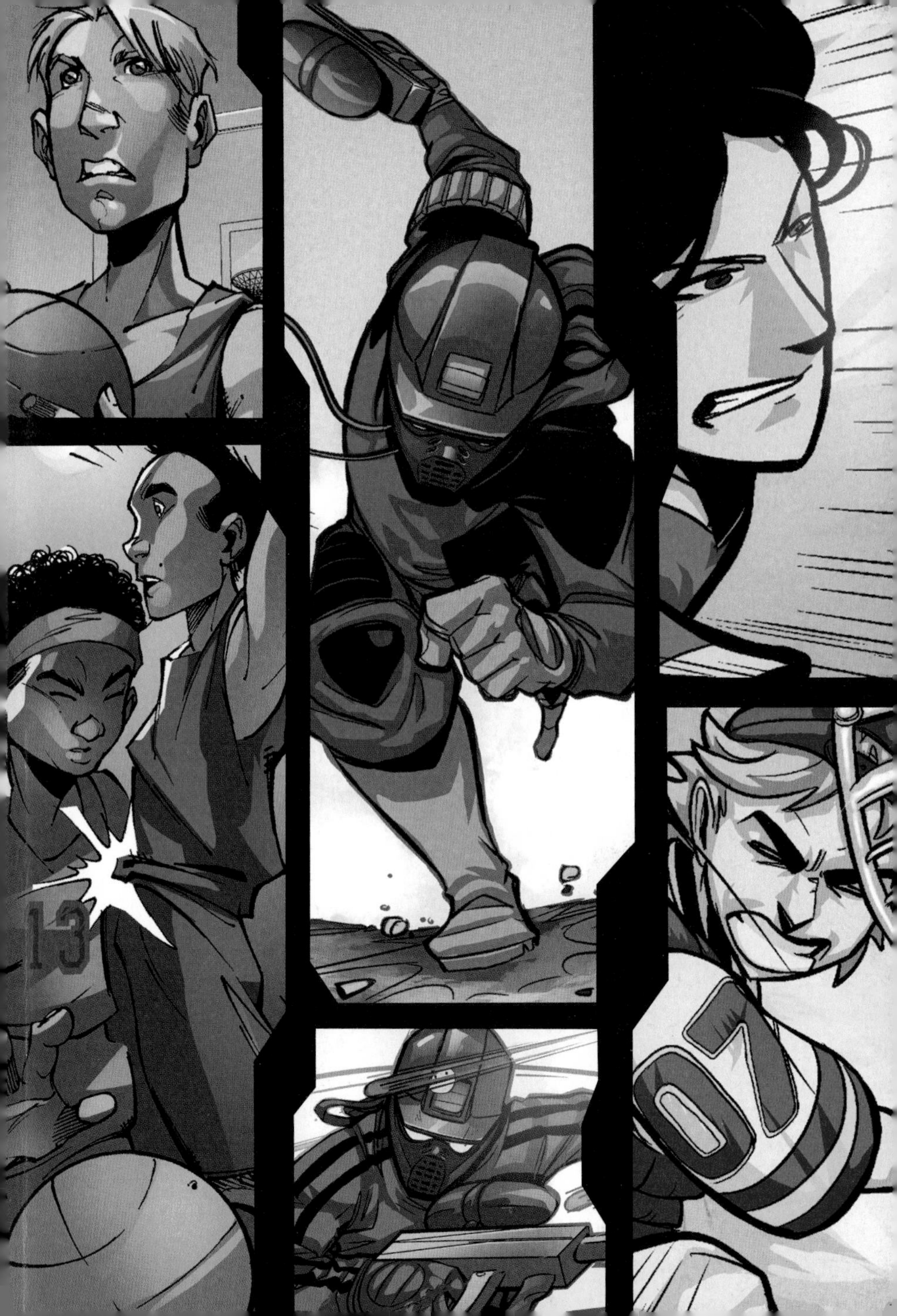

# UP NEXT ›››

on Sports Illustrated KIDS

:02 SPORTS ZONE SPECIAL REPORT

:04 FEATURE PRESENTATION:

# REALITY CHECK

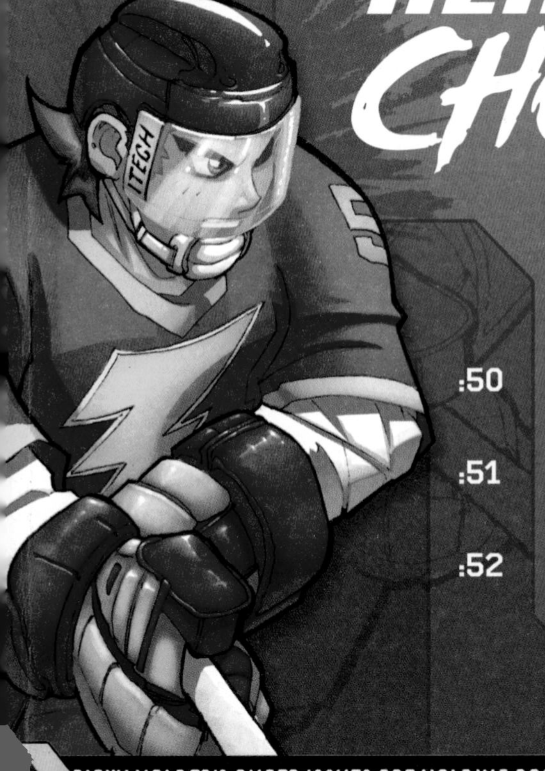

FOLLOWED BY:

:50 SPORTS ZONE POSTGAME RECAP

:51 SPORTS ZONE POSTGAME EXTRA

:52 SI KIDS INFO CENTER

RICKY HOLDER'S ANGER ISSUES ARE HOLDING BACK THE BLITZ THIS SEASO

SIK TICKER

# SPORTS ZONE

## SPECIAL REPORT

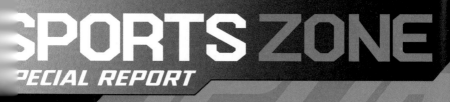

# BLITZ TEAM TO HOLDER: "DON'T SKATE ANGRY, RICKY!"

BLITZ

5
5

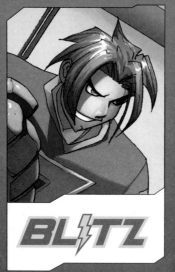

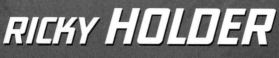

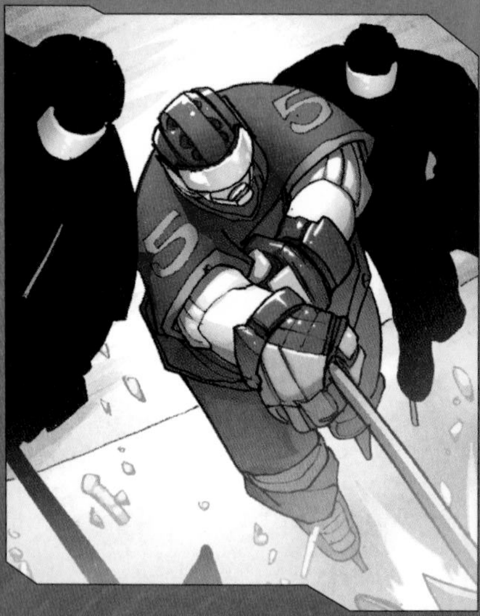

# RICKY HOLDER

**STATS:**

**AGE:** 14

TEAM: BLITZ

**NUMBER:** 05

**POSITION:** DEFENSEMAN

**BIO:** Ricky Holder is the Blitz's best defensive player, but lately he's been all offense — and not the goal-scoring kind. Ricky's been spending more time in the penalty box than in the game, and his anger issues have put him on thin ice with his teammates. To make matters worse, Ricky's father continues to pressure Ricky to play rough, leaving the teen between the puck and a hard place.

# JENNIFER TAYLOR

**TEAM:** BLITZ
**AGE:** 14 **NUMBER:** 09
**TEAM ROLE:** CAPTAIN
**POSITION:** CENTER
**BIO:** Jen is far and away the best center in the entire state. She leads the league in assists and total points earned. It's no surprise she is the Blitz's team captain.

BLZ vs BKS
3-1
TGR vs ROR
33-32
EAG vs BAN
14-7
SPA vs WLD
4-3
BAN vs ROR
21-15
ROR vs LIG
4-3
BLZ vs WLS

## JACK HOLDER

**TEAM:** BLITZ **AGE:** 44
**BIO:** Mr. Holder is Ricky's father. He pushes his son to play hard and be aggressive at all times — even during practice scrimmages.

**MR. HOLDER**

## MARK JACOBS

**TEAM:** BLITZ **AGE:** 13 **NO:** 17 **POSITION:** LEFT WING
**BIO:** Mark Jacobs is a top-notch forward. He's skilled, works hard, shares the puck, and is well-liked among his teammates.

**JACOBS**

## MICHAEL MORELLI

**TEAM:** BLITZ **AGE:** 42 **POSITION:** COACH
**BIO:** Michael Morelli is a no-nonsense hockey coach who stands for hard work, smart play — and, above all else, team unity.

**COACH**

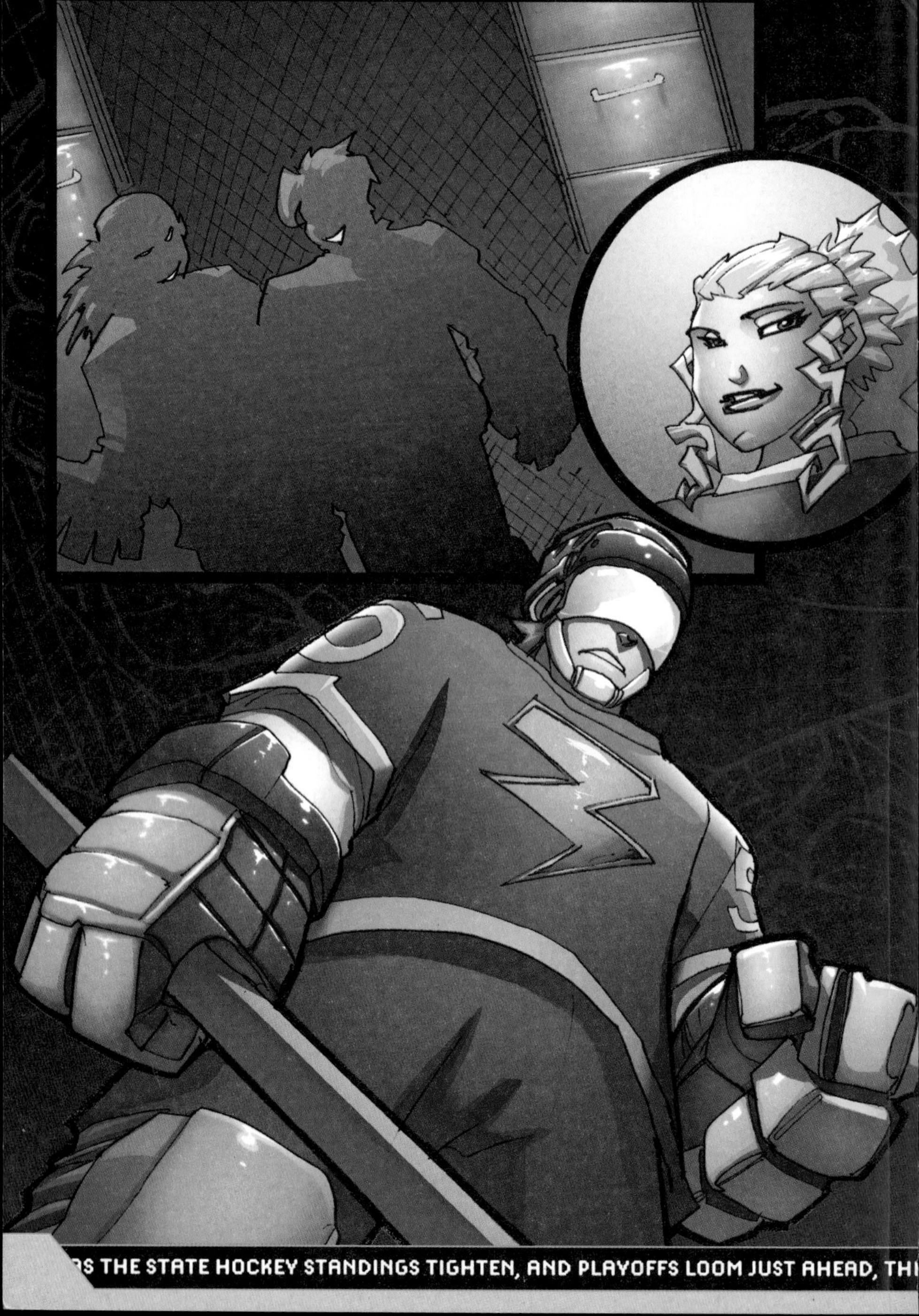
AS THE STATE HOCKEY STANDINGS TIGHTEN, AND PLAYOFFS LOOM JUST AHEAD, TH

**Sports Illustrated KIDS**

*PRESENTS*

# REALITY CHECK

*A PRODUCTION OF*

**STONE ARCH BOOKS**
a capstone imprint

written by *Nel Yomtov*
illustrated by *Gerardo Sandoval*
colored by *Benny Fuentes*

designed and directed by *Bob Lentz*
edited by *Sean Tulien*
creative direction by *Heather Kindseth*
editorial direction by *Michael Dahl*

Sports Illustrated Kids *Reality Check* is published by Stone Arch Books,
1710 Roe Crest Drive,
North Mankato, Minnesota 56003.
www.capstonepub.com

Summary: When he's playing hockey, Ricky Holder hits hard and never
holds back. During a scrimmage, Ricky injures his own team's top scorer.
Ricky's father is proud of him, but his teammates ditch him because of his
dangerous checks. Ricky tries to ease up a little, but his teammates won't
forgive him, and his father is mad that he's not playing aggressively. Can
Ricky fix things before the state's toughest team comes to town?

Cataloging-in-Publication data is available on the Library of Congress
website.

ISBN: 978-1-4342-1912-1 (library binding)
ISBN: 978-1-4342-2294-7 (paperback)

Printed in the United States of America in Stevens Point, Wisconsin.
012012   006569R

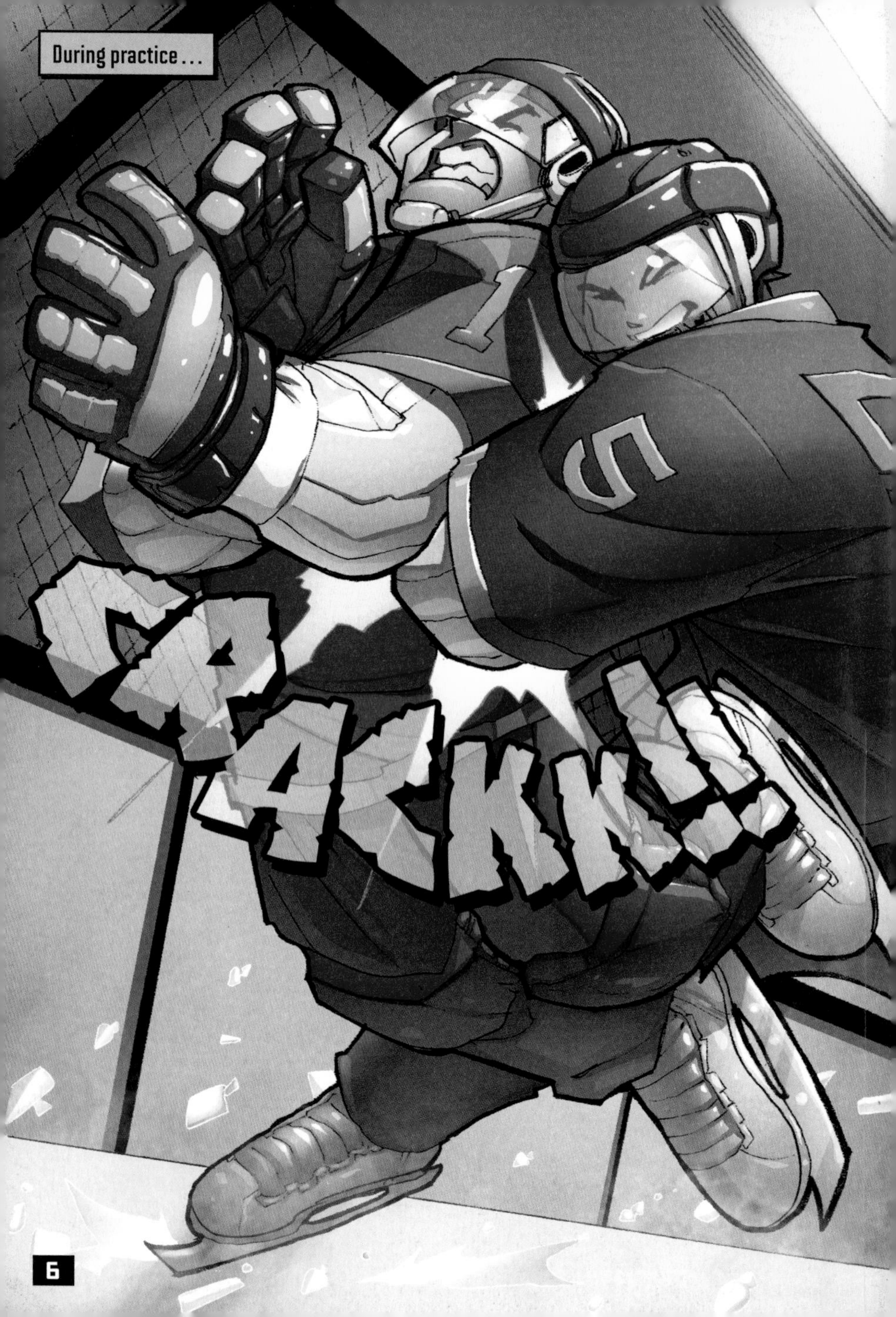
During practice . . .
CRACK!!

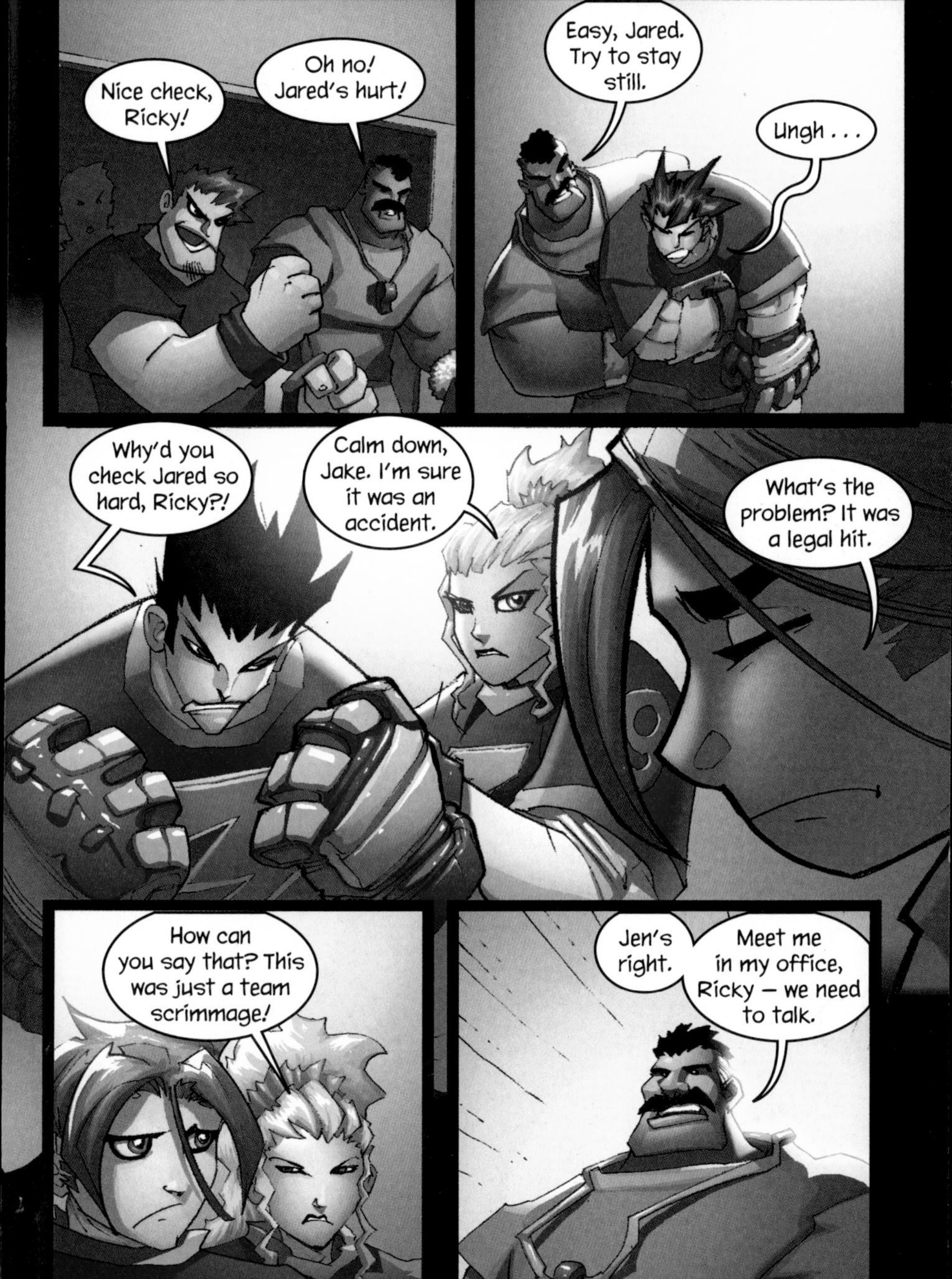

Nice check, Ricky!
Oh no! Jared's hurt!
Easy, Jared. Try to stay still.
Ungh . . .
Why'd you check Jared so hard, Ricky?!
Calm down, Jake. I'm sure it was an accident.
What's the problem? It was a legal hit.
How can you say that? This was just a team scrimmage!
Jen's right.
Meet me in my office, Ricky — we need to talk.

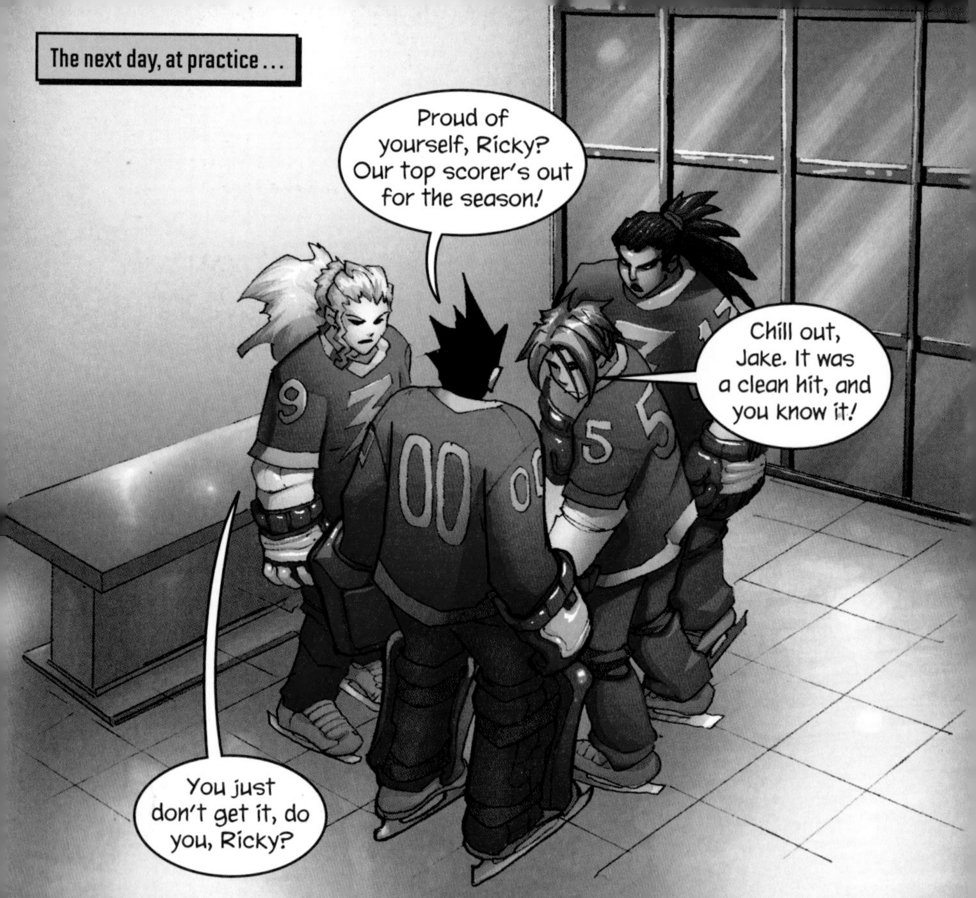
The next day, at practice . . .
Proud of yourself, Ricky? Our top scorer's out for the season!
Chill out, Jake. It was a clean hit, and you know it!
You just don't get it, do you, Ricky?

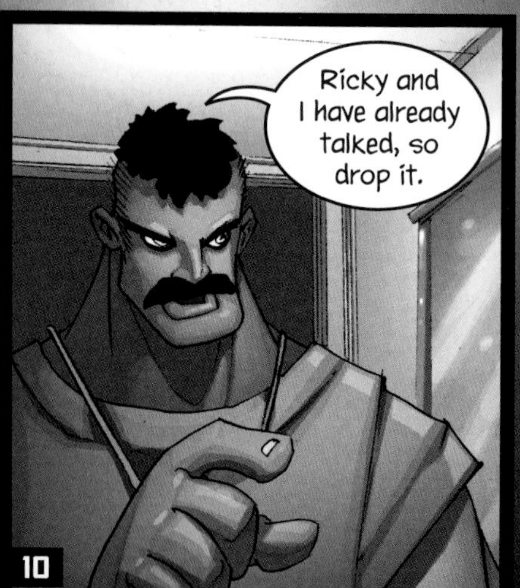
Ricky and I have already talked, so drop it.

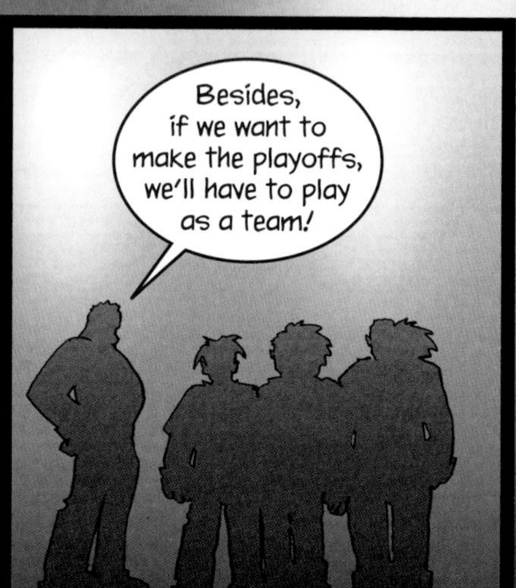
Besides, if we want to make the playoffs, we'll have to play as a team!

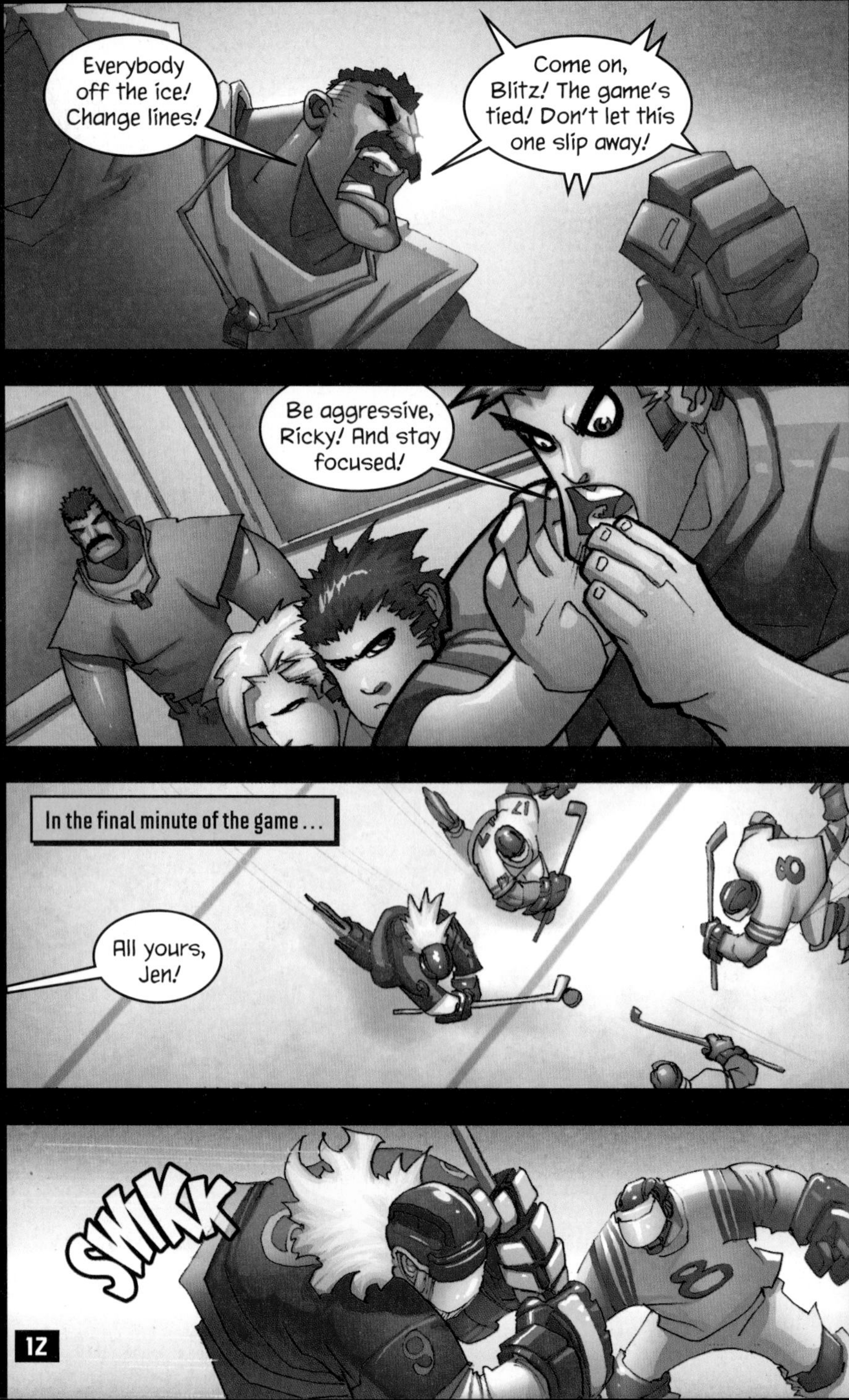
Everybody off the ice! Change lines!
Come on, Blitz! The game's tied! Don't let this one slip away!
Be aggressive, Ricky! And stay focused!
In the final minute of the game . . .
All yours, Jen!
SWIKK

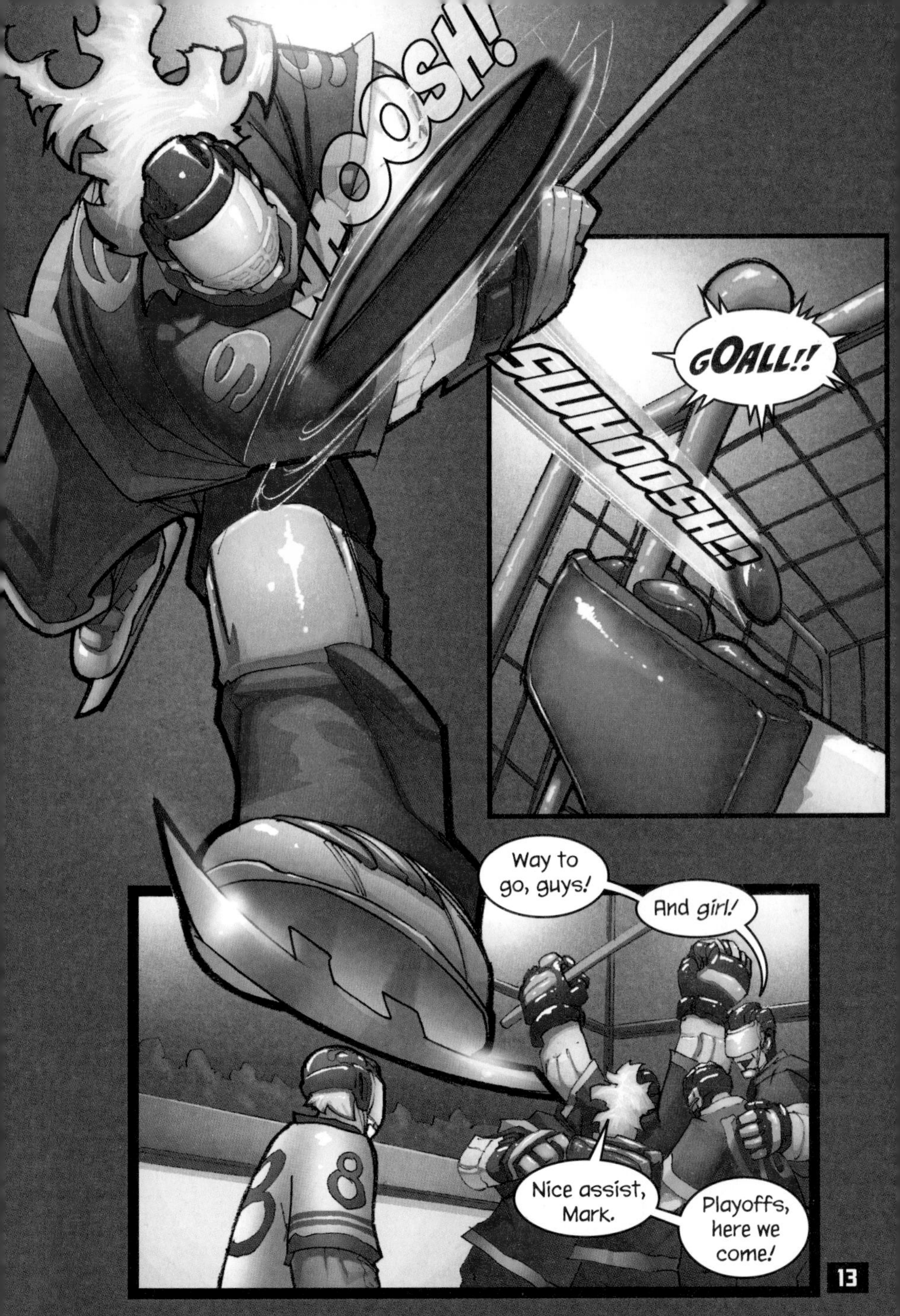
WHOOSH!
SWOOSH!
GOALL!!
Way to go, guys!
And girl!
Nice assist, Mark.
Playoffs, here we come!

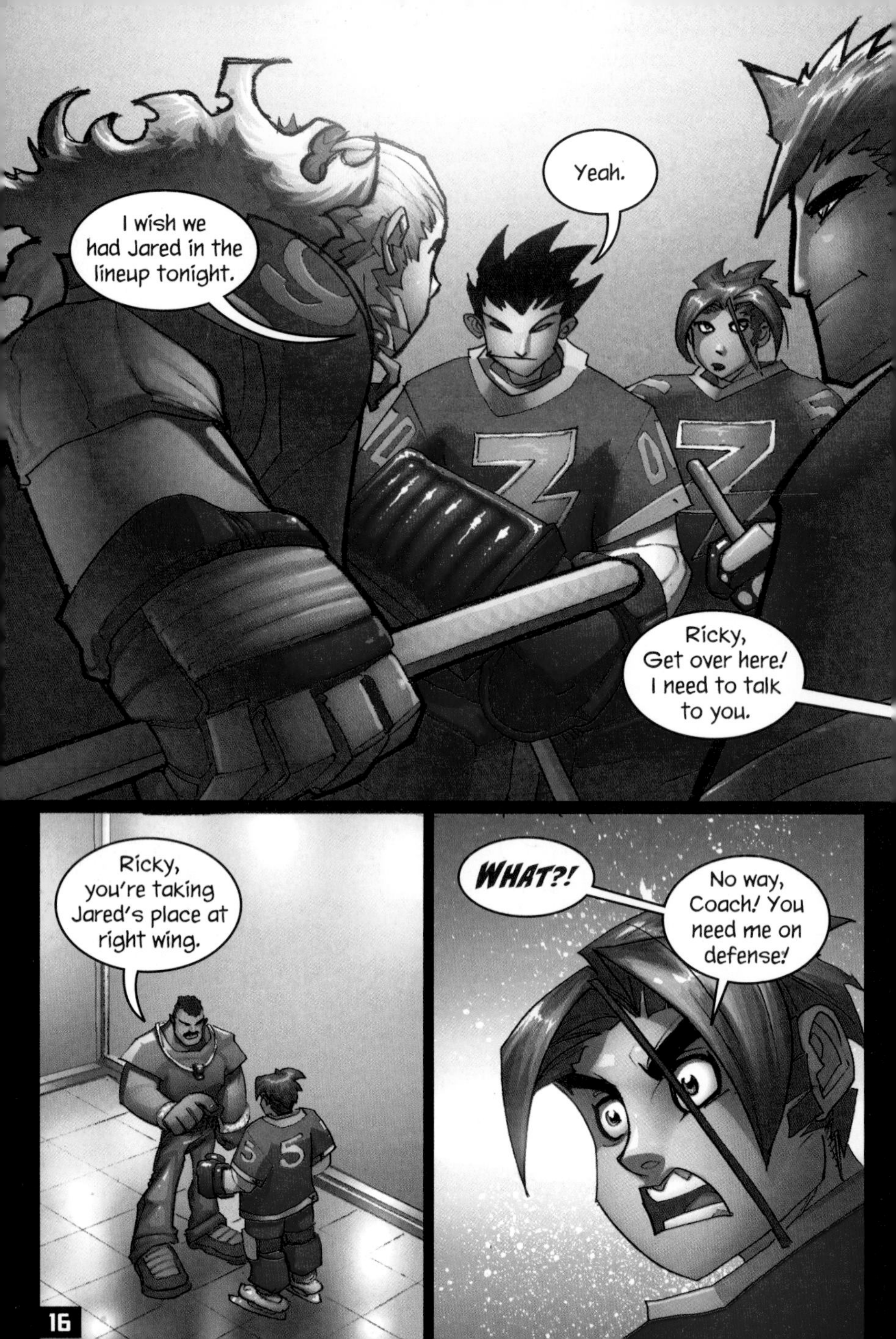
I wish we had Jared in the lineup tonight.
Yeah.
Ricky, Get over here! I need to talk to you.
Ricky, you're taking Jared's place at right wing.
WHAT?!
No way, Coach! You need me on defense!

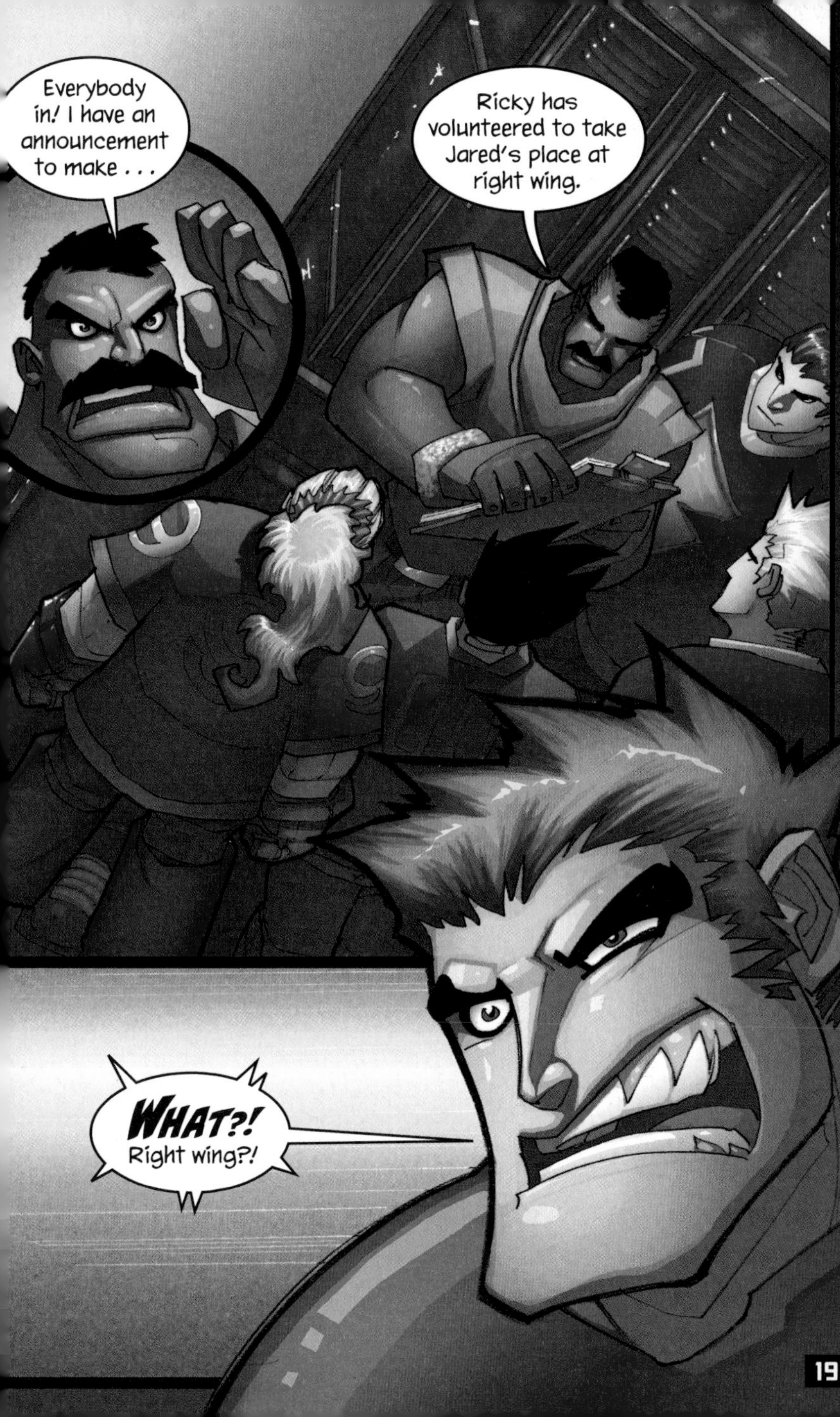

Everybody in! I have an announcement to make . . .
Ricky has volunteered to take Jared's place at right wing.
WHAT?! Right wing?!

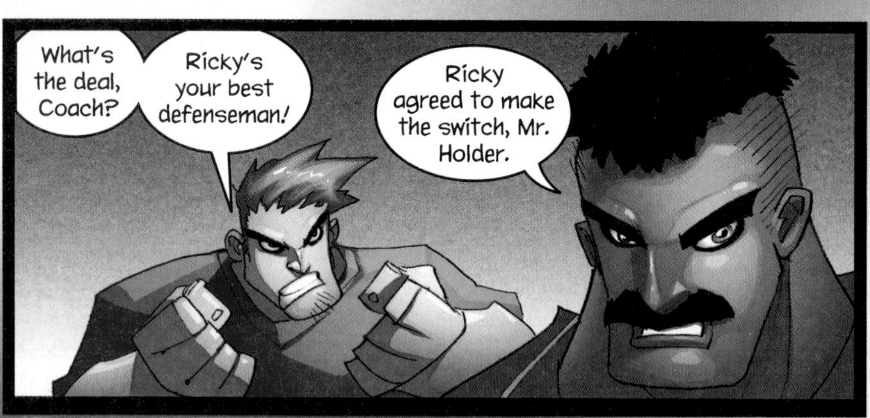
What's the deal, Coach?
Ricky's your best defenseman!
Ricky agreed to make the switch, Mr. Holder.

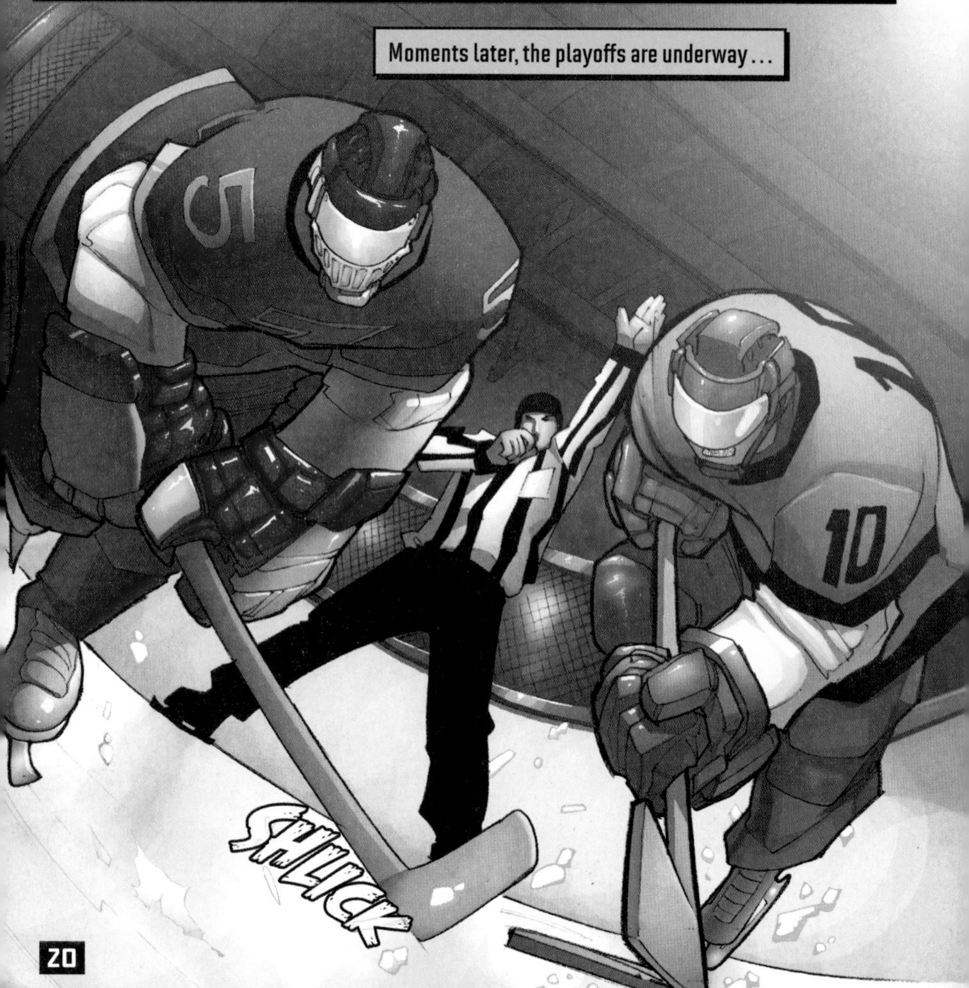
Moments later, the playoffs are underway . . .
5
10
SHLICK

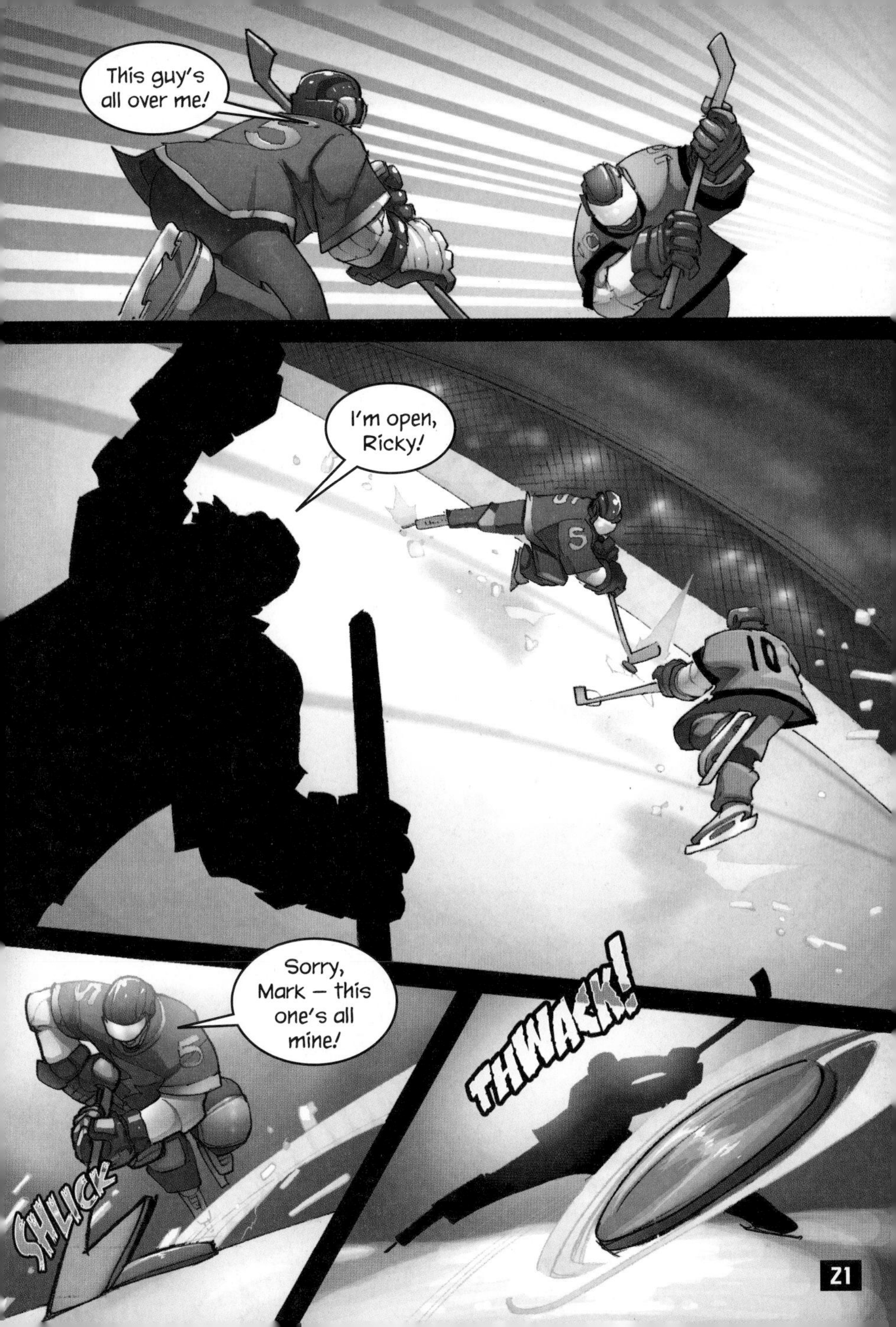
This guy's all over me!
I'm open, Ricky!
Sorry, Mark — this one's all mine!
SHLICK
THWACK!

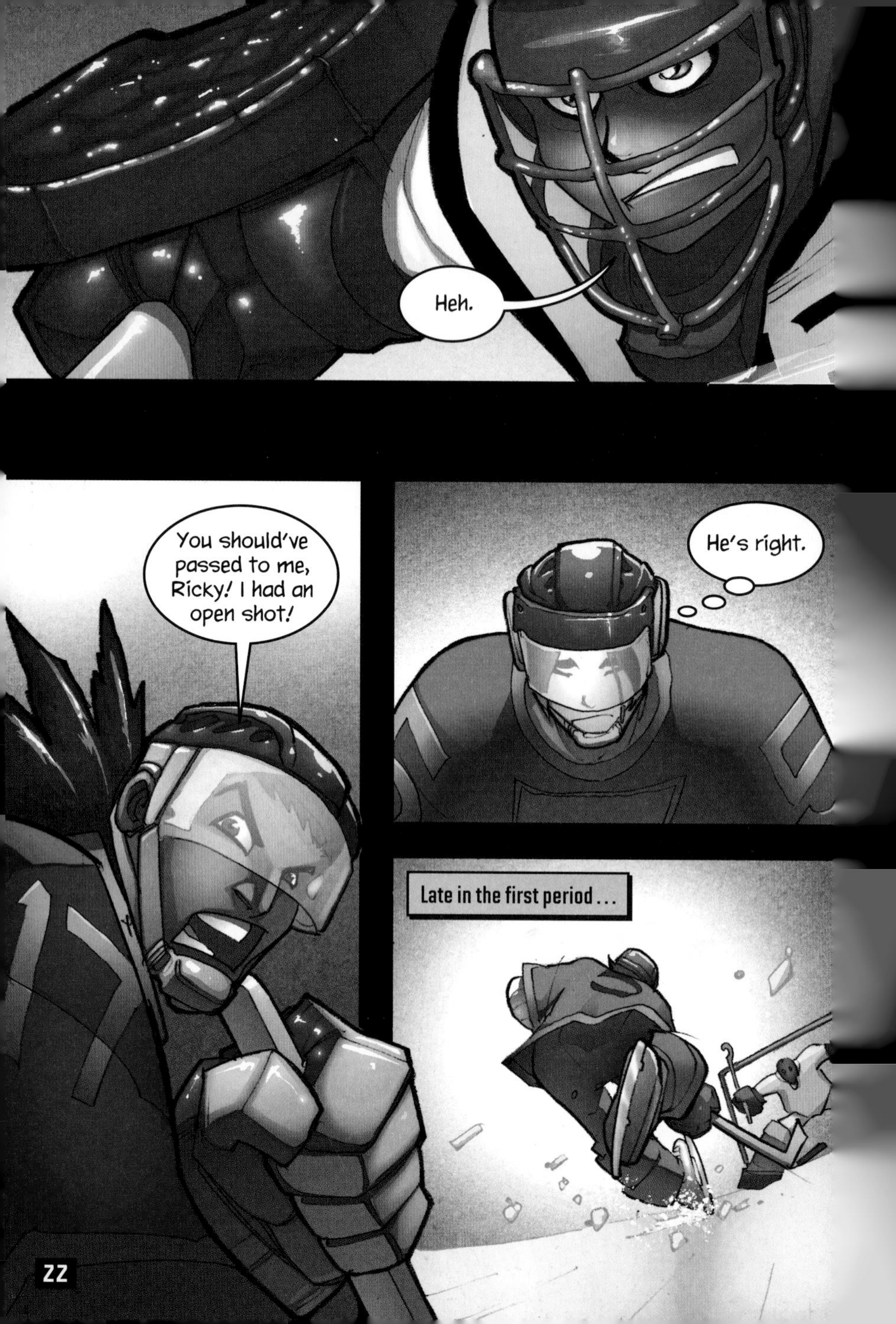

Heh.
You should've passed to me, Ricky! I had an open shot!
He's right.
Late in the first period . . .

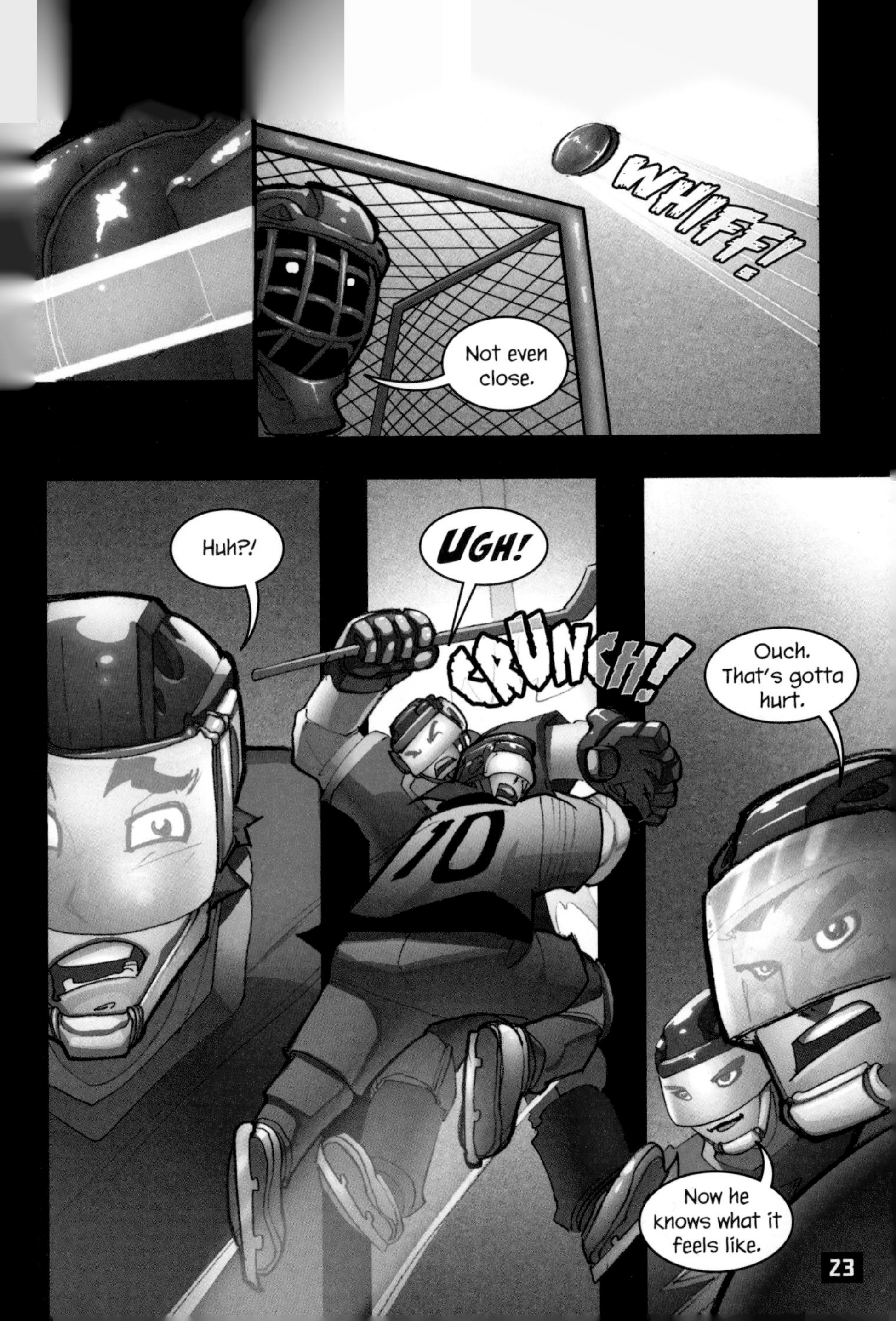
WHIFF!
Not even close.
Huh?!
UGH!
CRUNCH!
Ouch. That's gotta hurt.
Now he knows what it feels like.

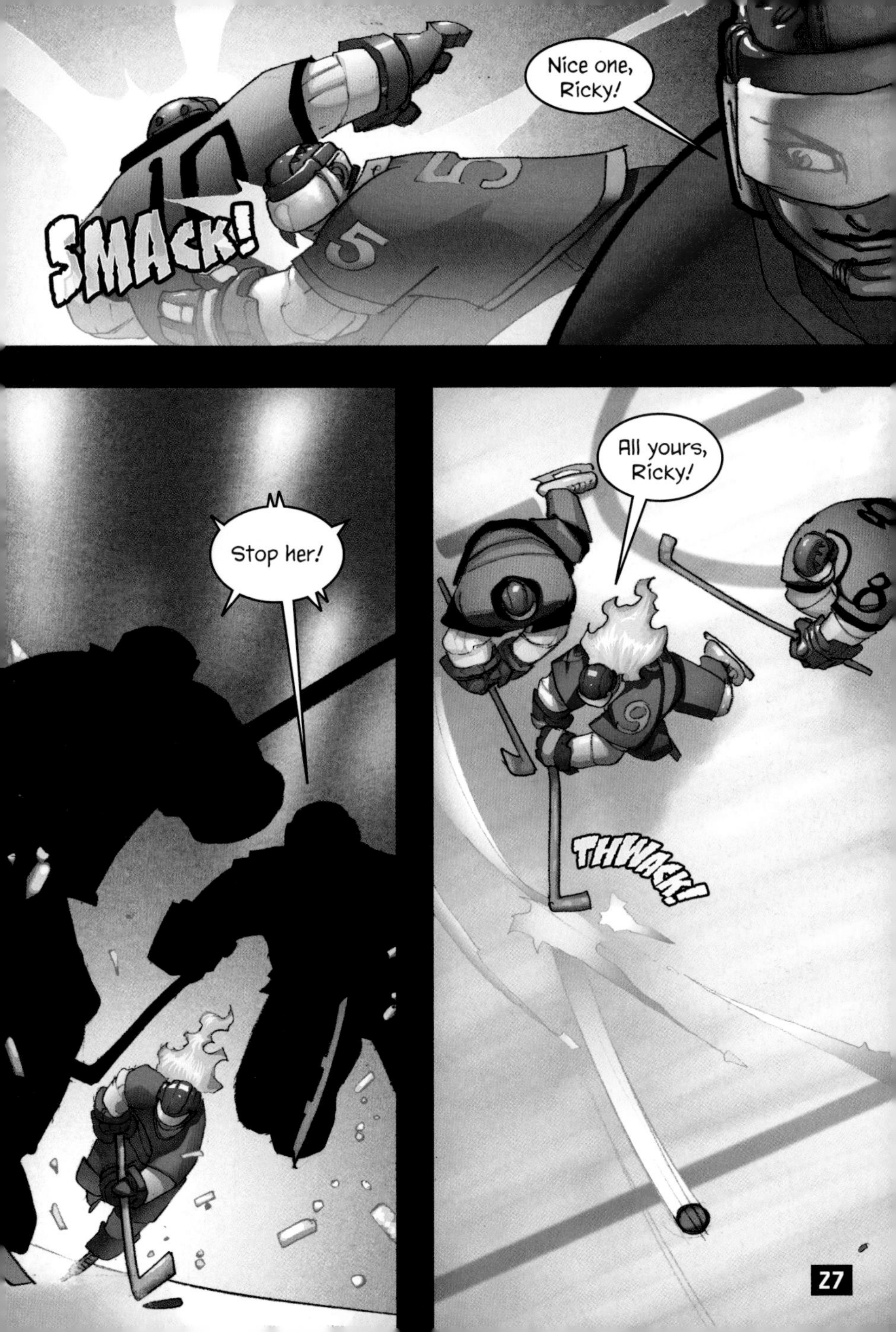
SMACK!
Nice one, Ricky!
Stop her!
All yours, Ricky!
THWACK!

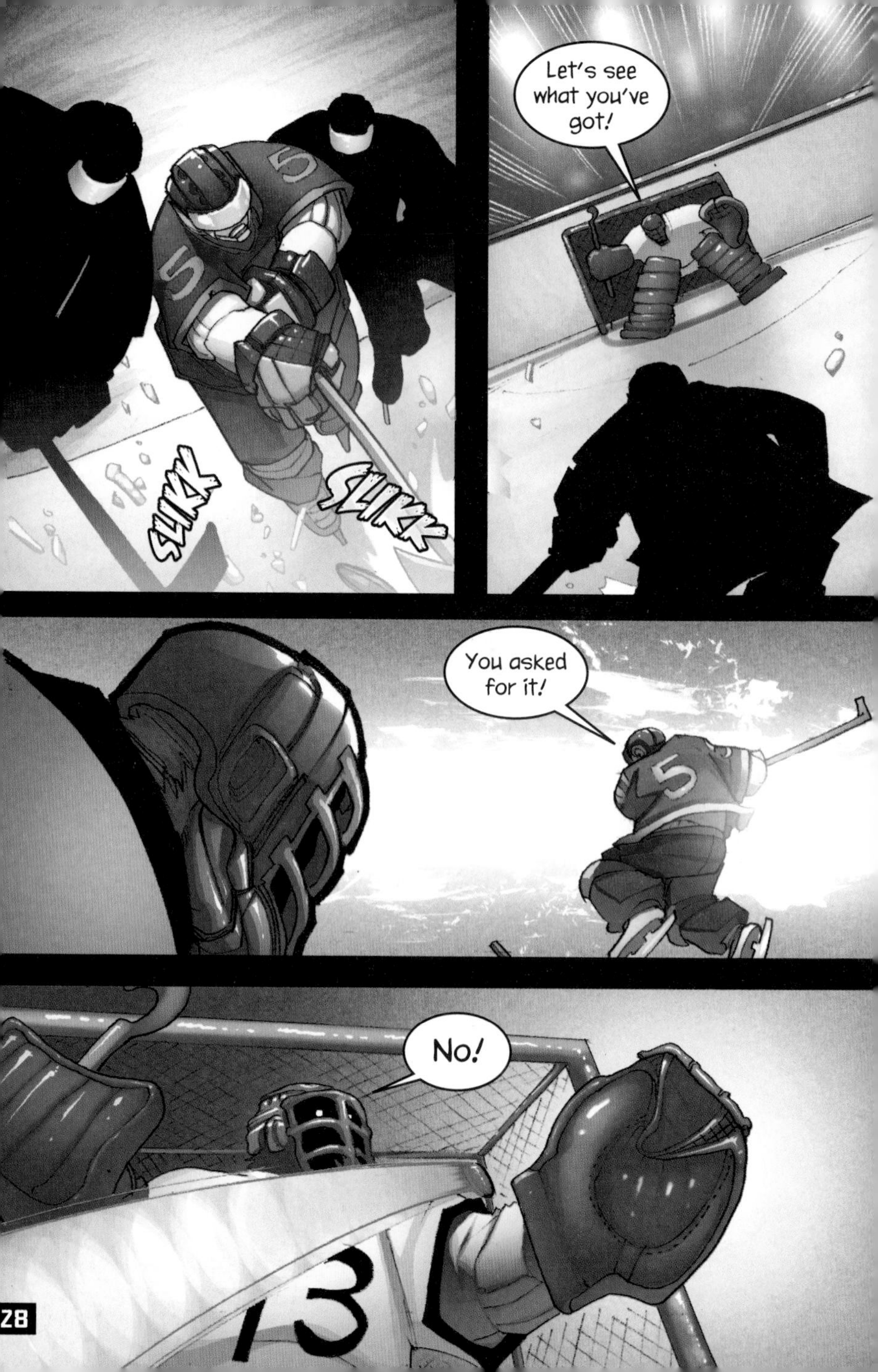
SLIKK
SLIKK
Let's see what you've got!
You asked for it!
No!

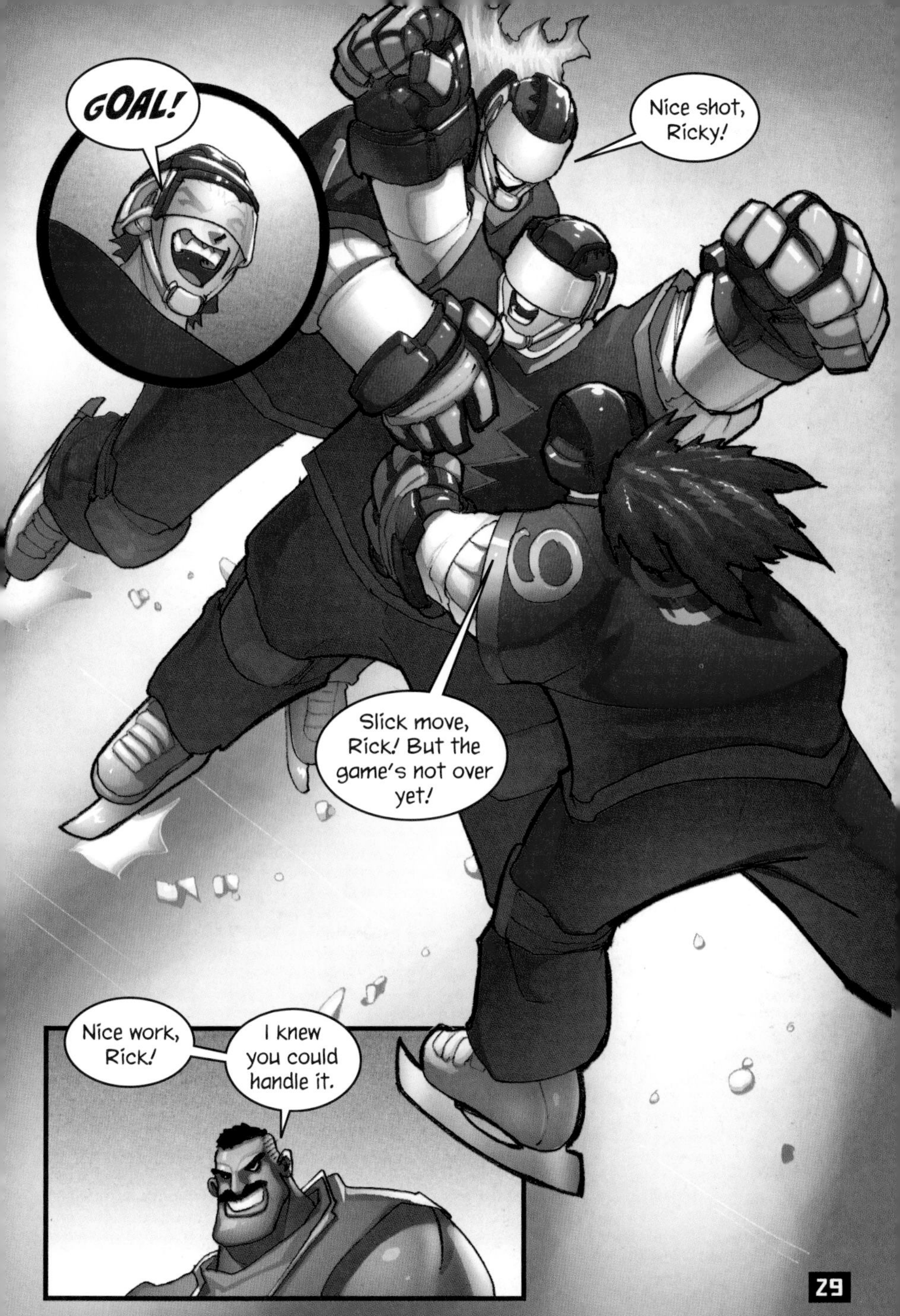

GOAL!
Nice shot, Ricky!
Slick move, Rick! But the game's not over yet!
Nice work, Rick!
I knew you could handle it.

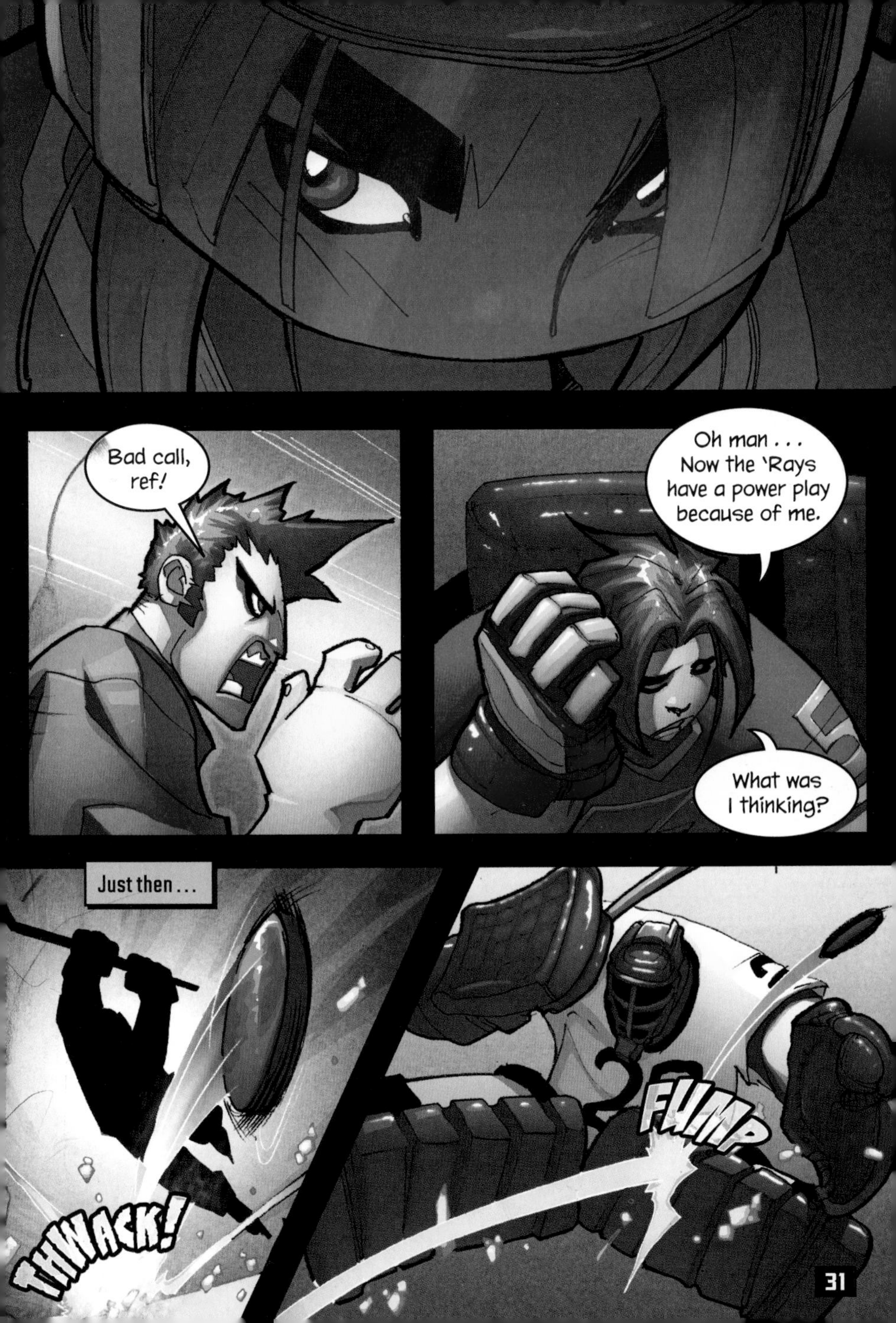
Bad call, ref!
Oh man . . . Now the 'Rays have a power play because of me.
What was I thinking?
Just then . . .
THWACK!
FUMP

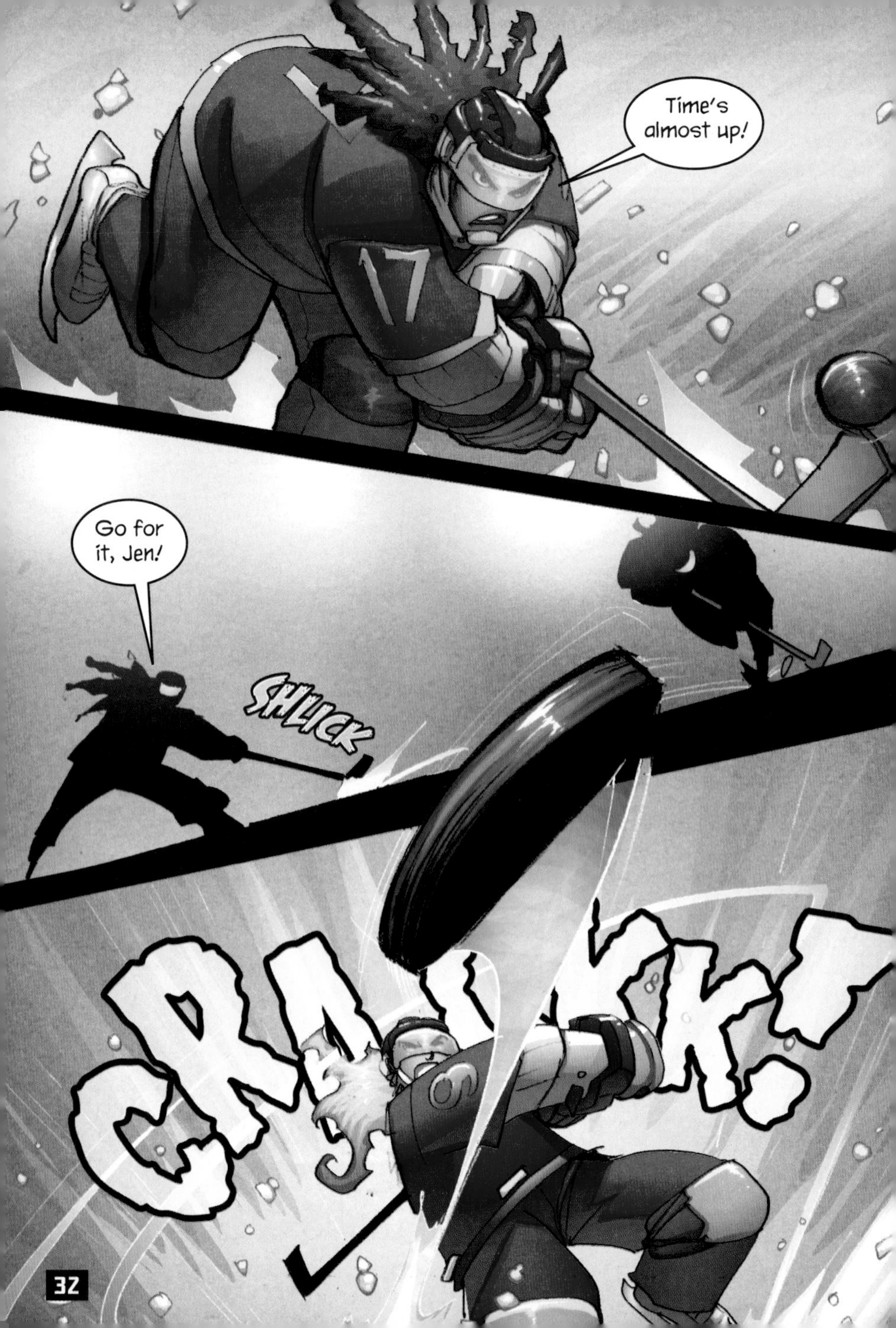
Time's almost up!
Go for it, Jen!
SHLICK
CRACK!

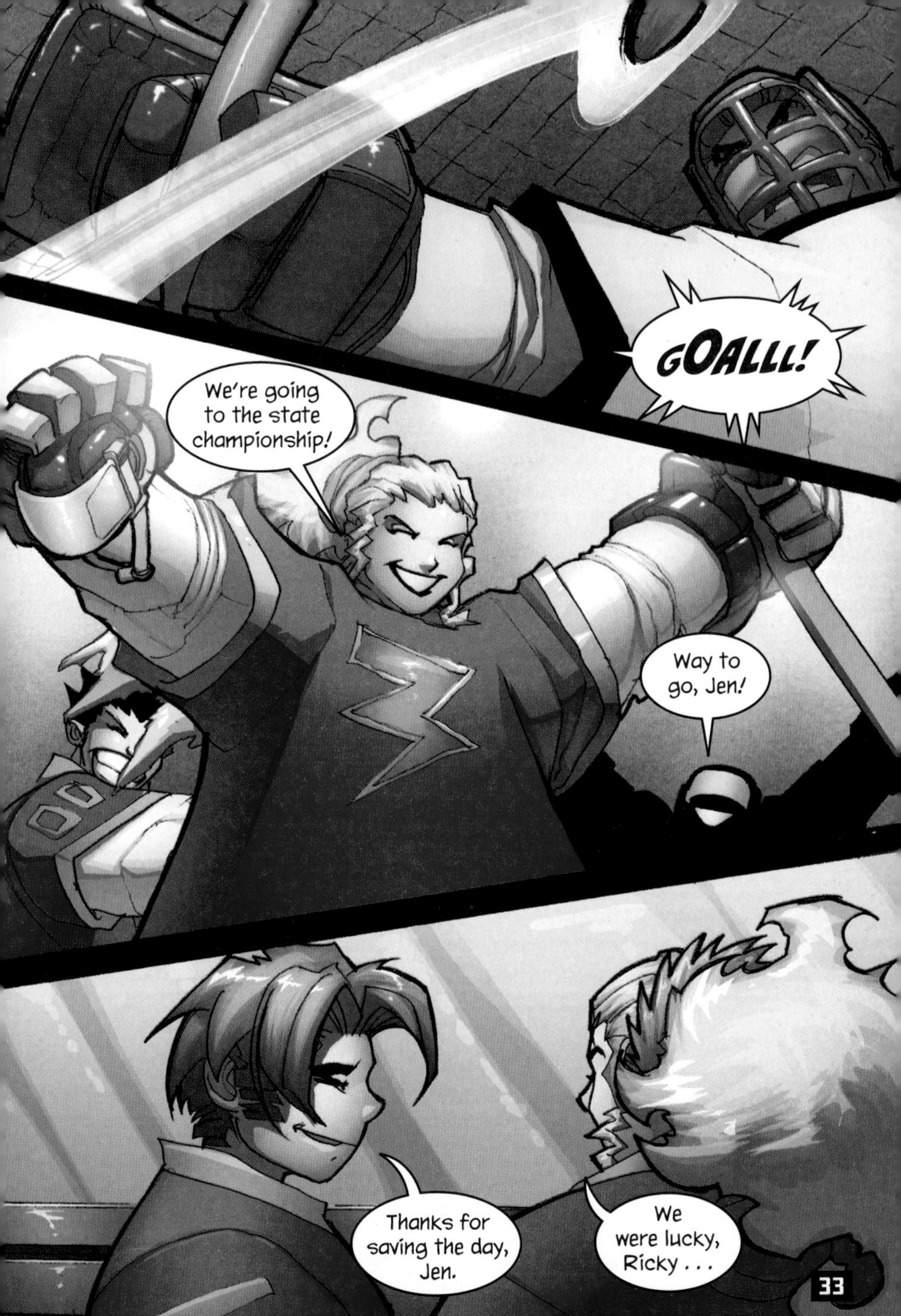
GOALLL!
We're going to the state championship!
Way to go, Jen!
Thanks for saving the day, Jen.
We were lucky, Ricky . . .

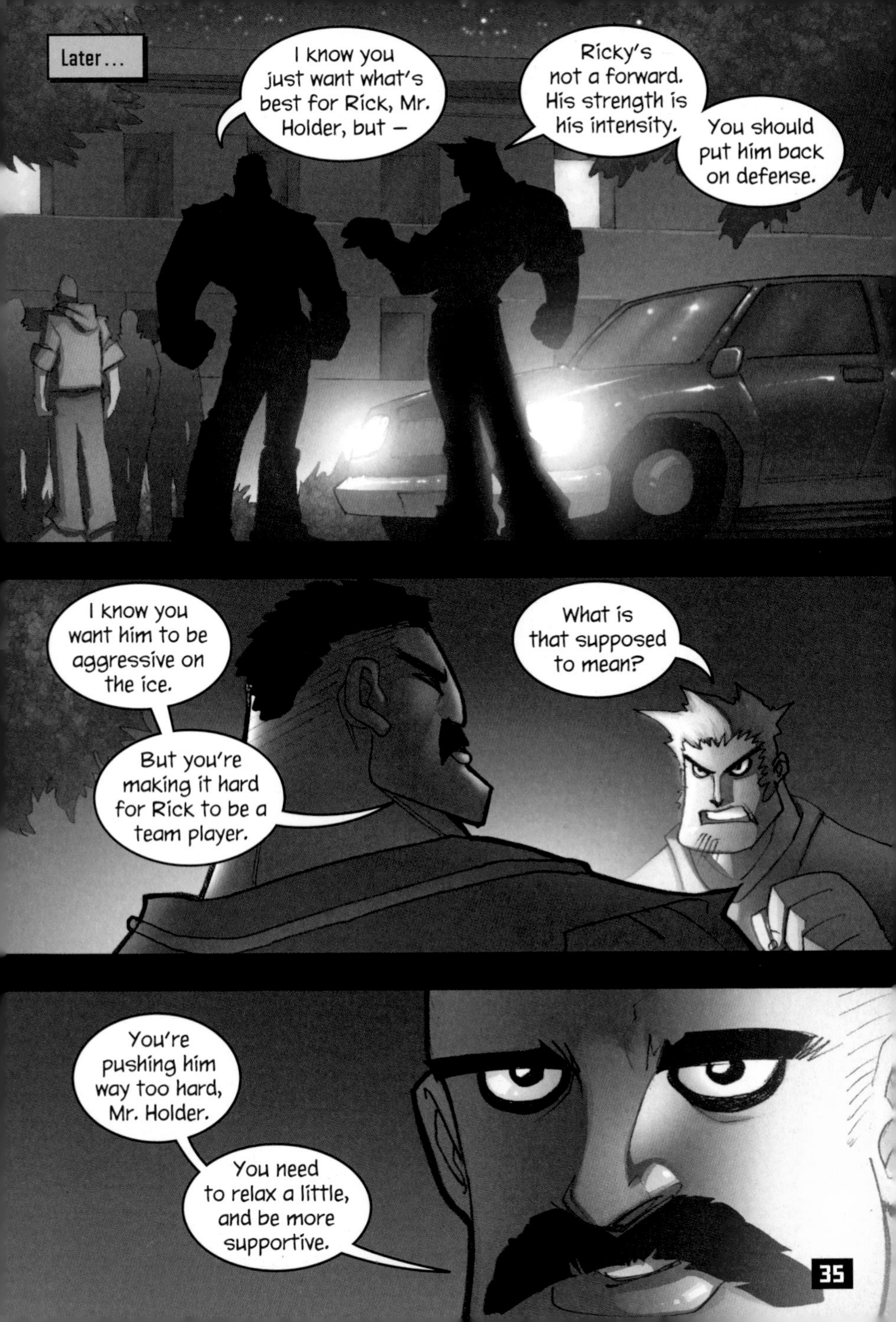
Later...
I know you just want what's best for Rick, Mr. Holder, but —
Ricky's not a forward. His strength is his intensity.
You should put him back on defense.
I know you want him to be aggressive on the ice.
But you're making it hard for Rick to be a team player.
What is that supposed to mean?
You're pushing him way too hard, Mr. Holder.
You need to relax a little, and be more supportive.

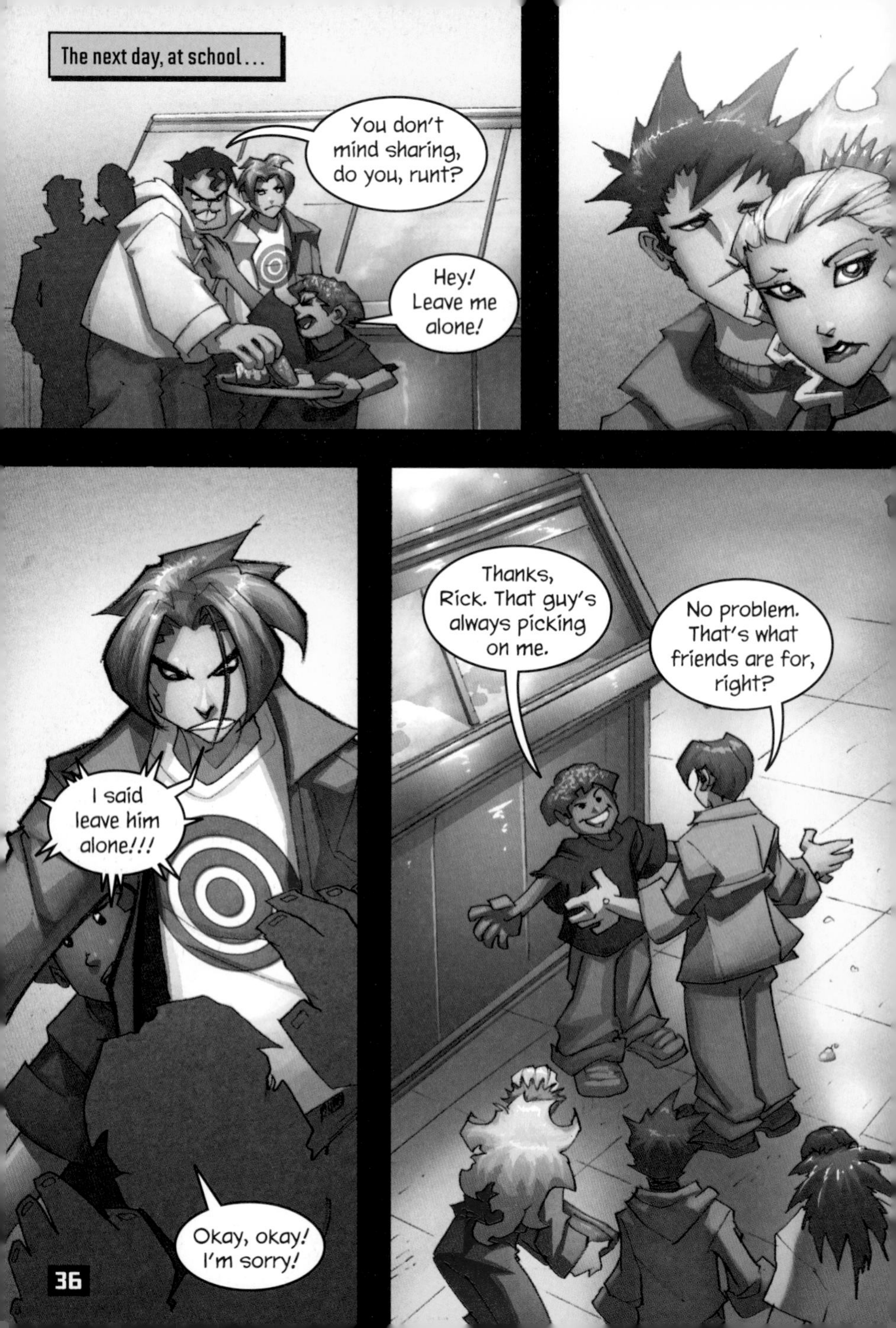
The next day, at school...
You don't mind sharing, do you, runt?
Hey! Leave me alone!
I said leave him alone!!!
Okay, okay! I'm sorry!
Thanks, Rick. That guy's always picking on me.
No problem. That's what friends are for, right?

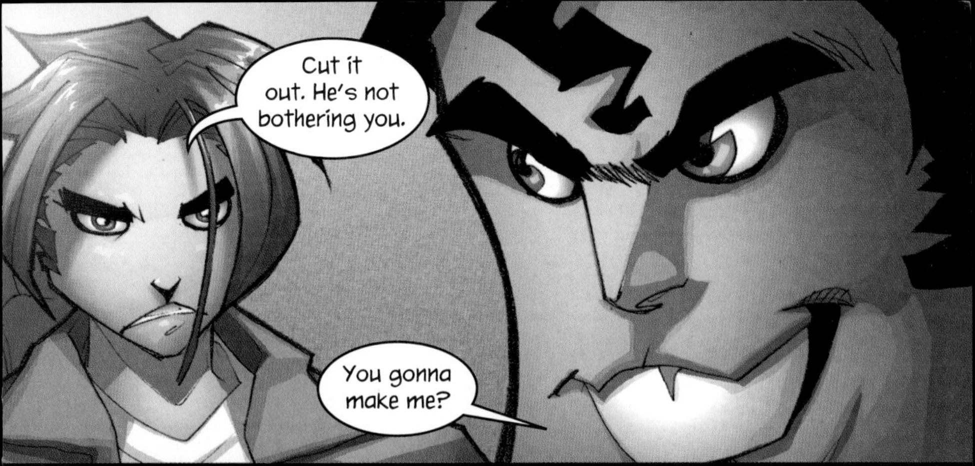
Cut it out. He's not bothering you.
You gonna make me?

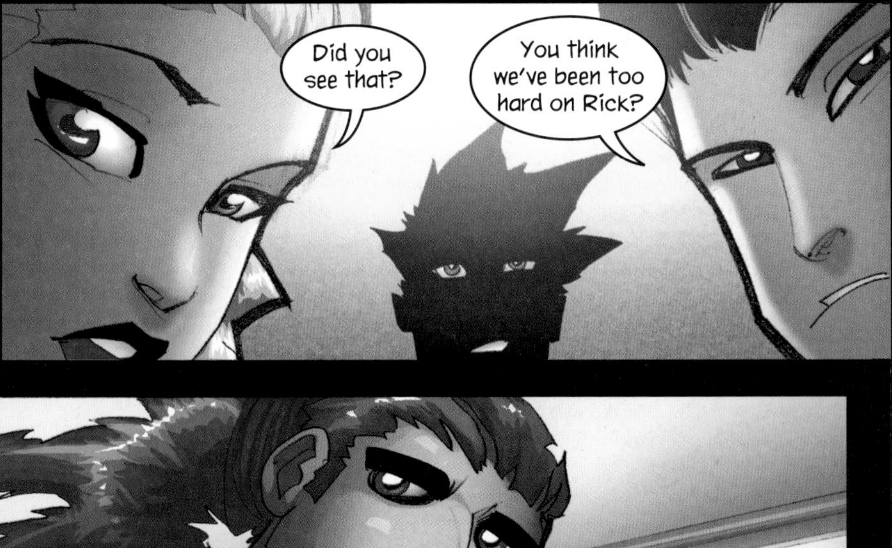
Did you see that?
You think we've been too hard on Rick?

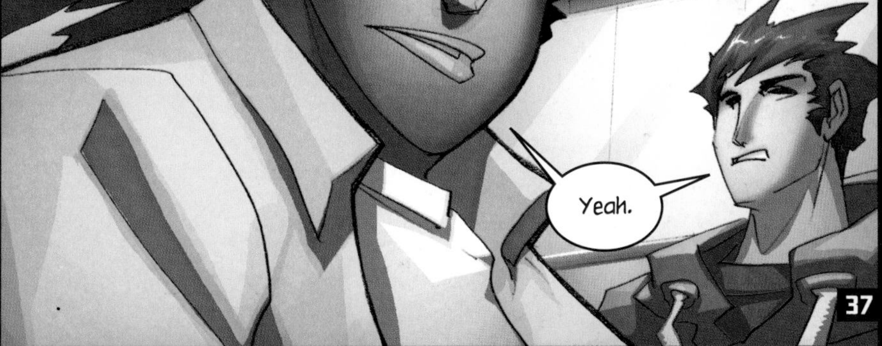
Yeah.

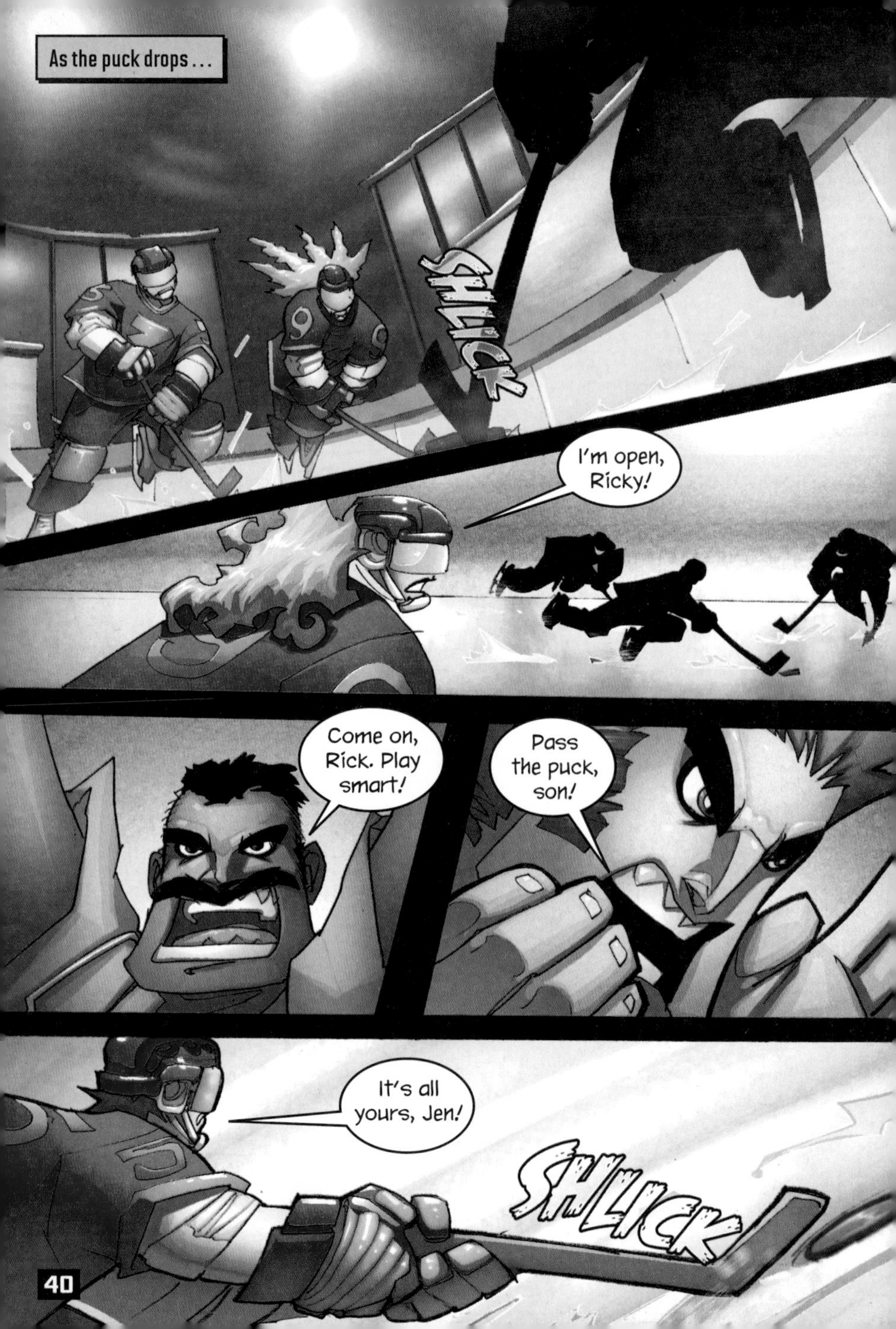
As the puck drops . . .
SHLICK
I'm open, Ricky!
Come on, Rick. Play smart!
Pass the puck, son!
It's all yours, Jen!
SHLICK

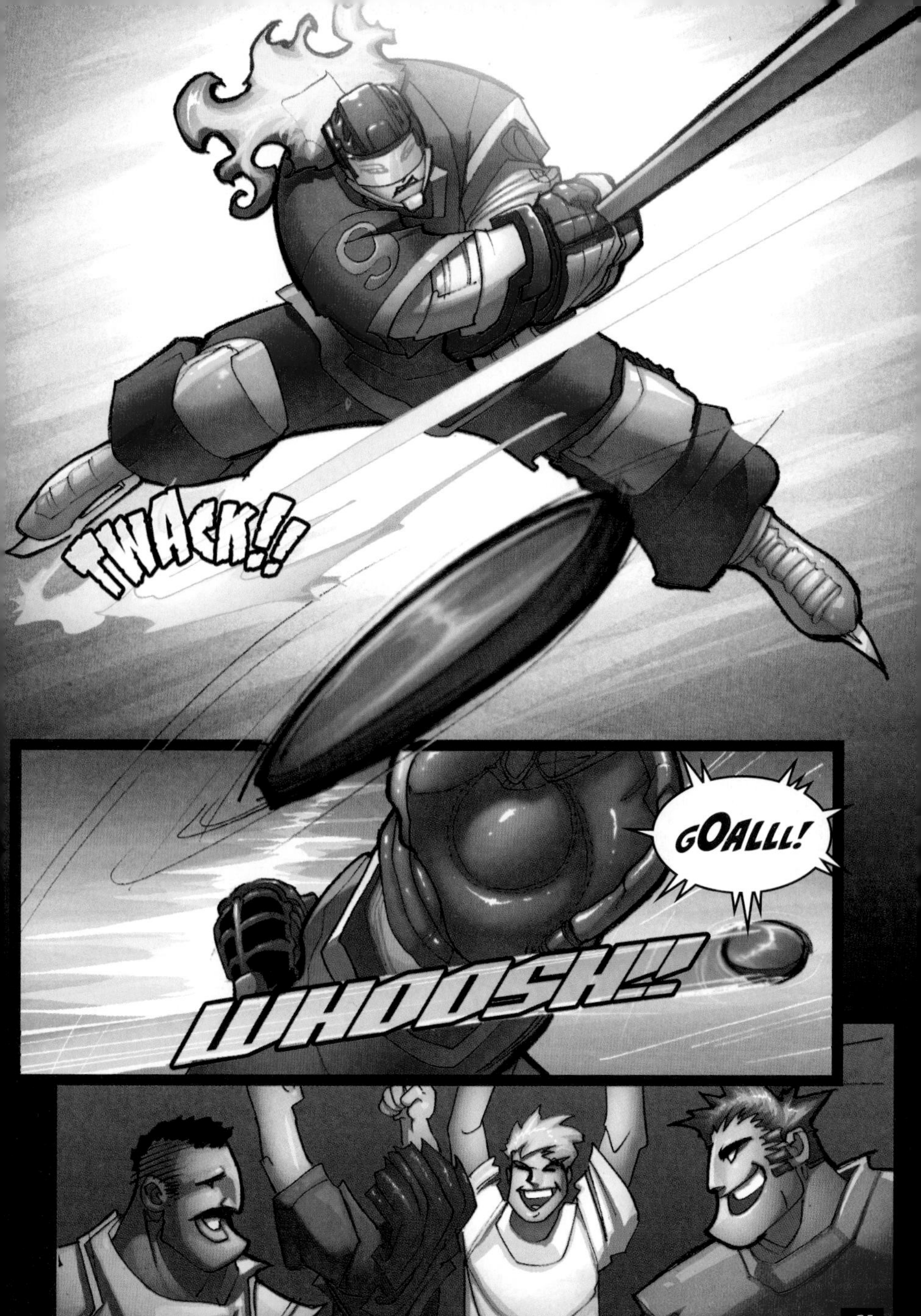
TWACK!!
GOALLL!
WHOOSH!!

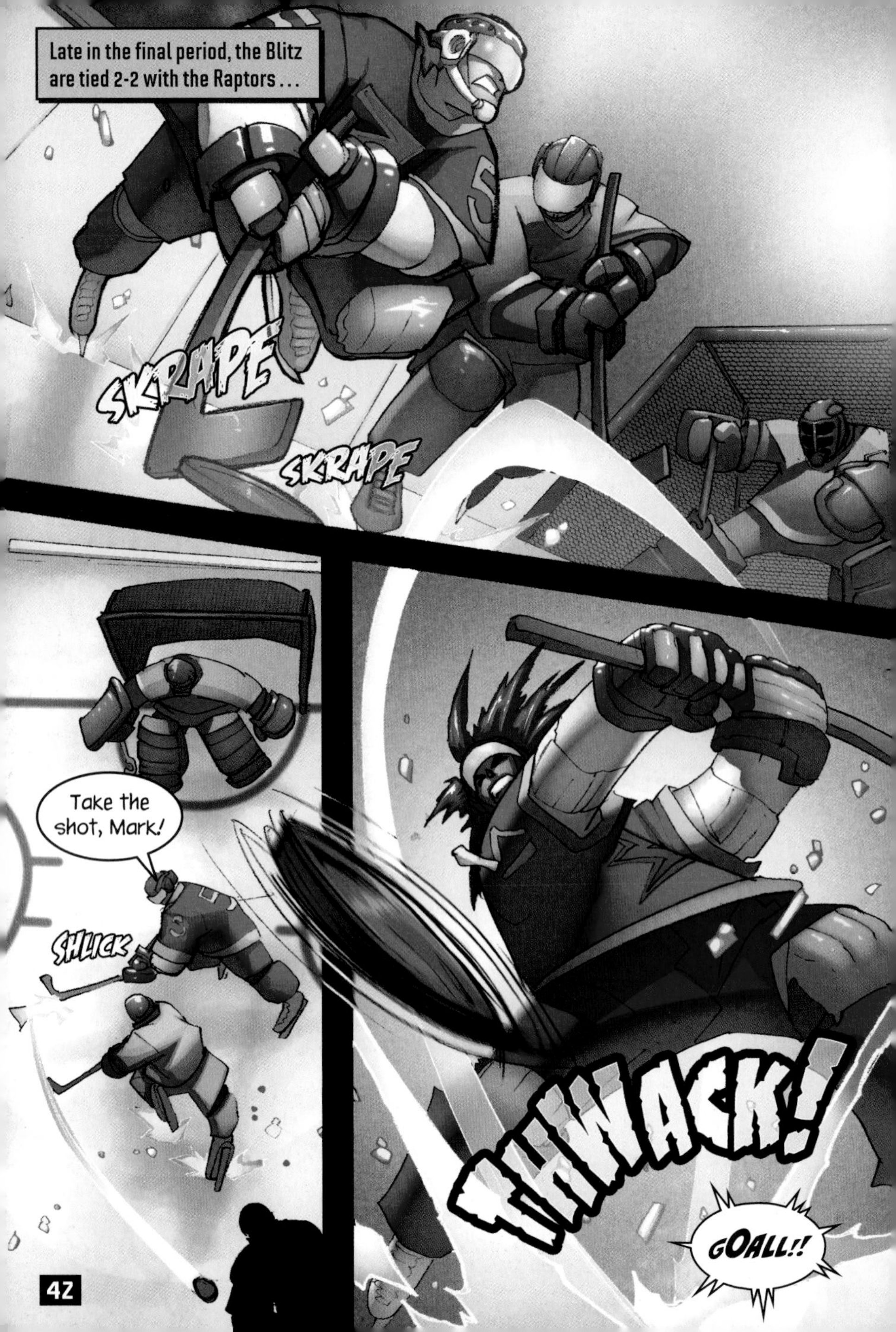
Late in the final period, the Blitz are tied 2-2 with the Raptors . . .
SKRAPE
SKRAPE
Take the shot, Mark!
SHLICK
THWACK!
GOALL!!

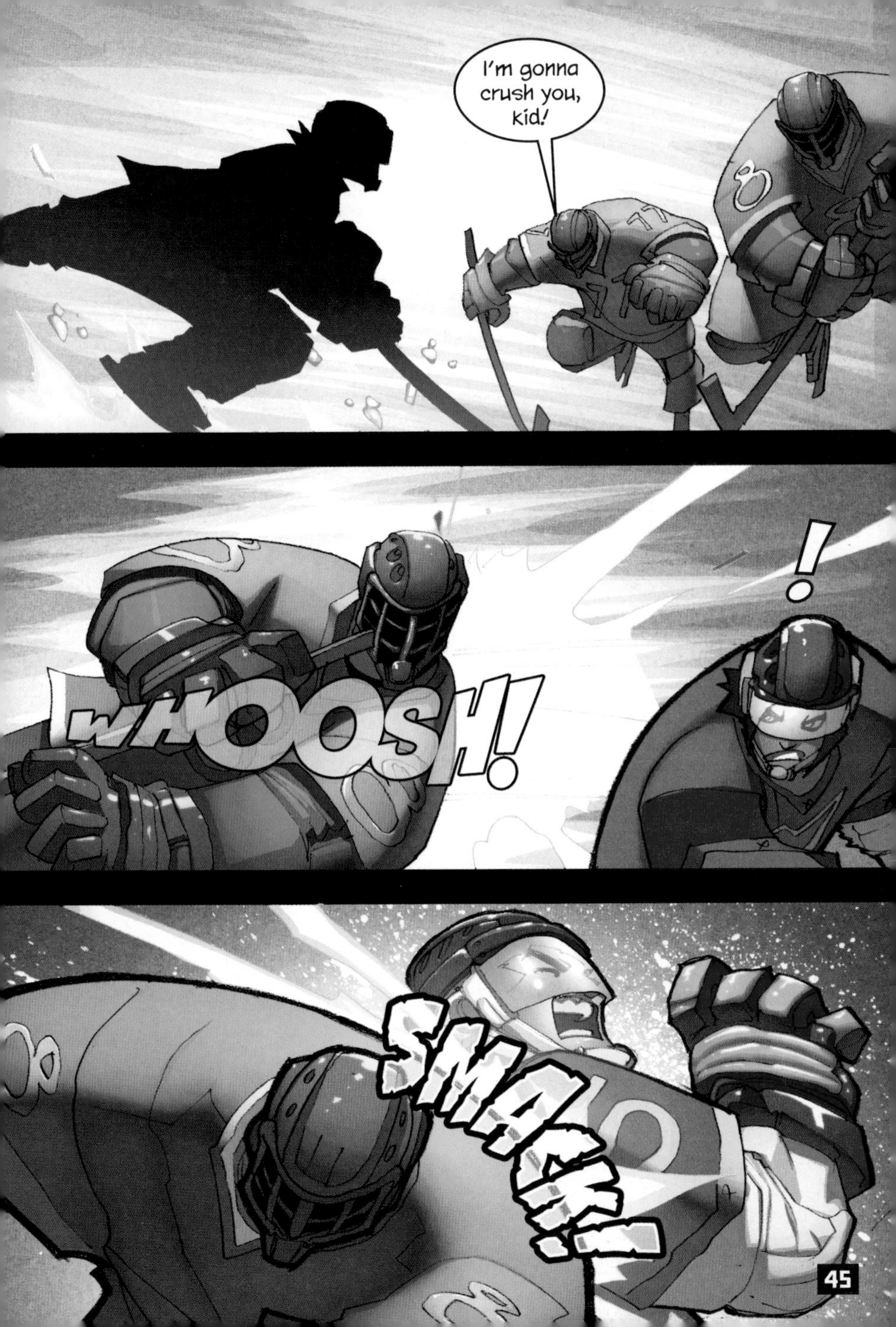
I'm gonna crush you, kid!
!
WHOOSH!
SMACK!!

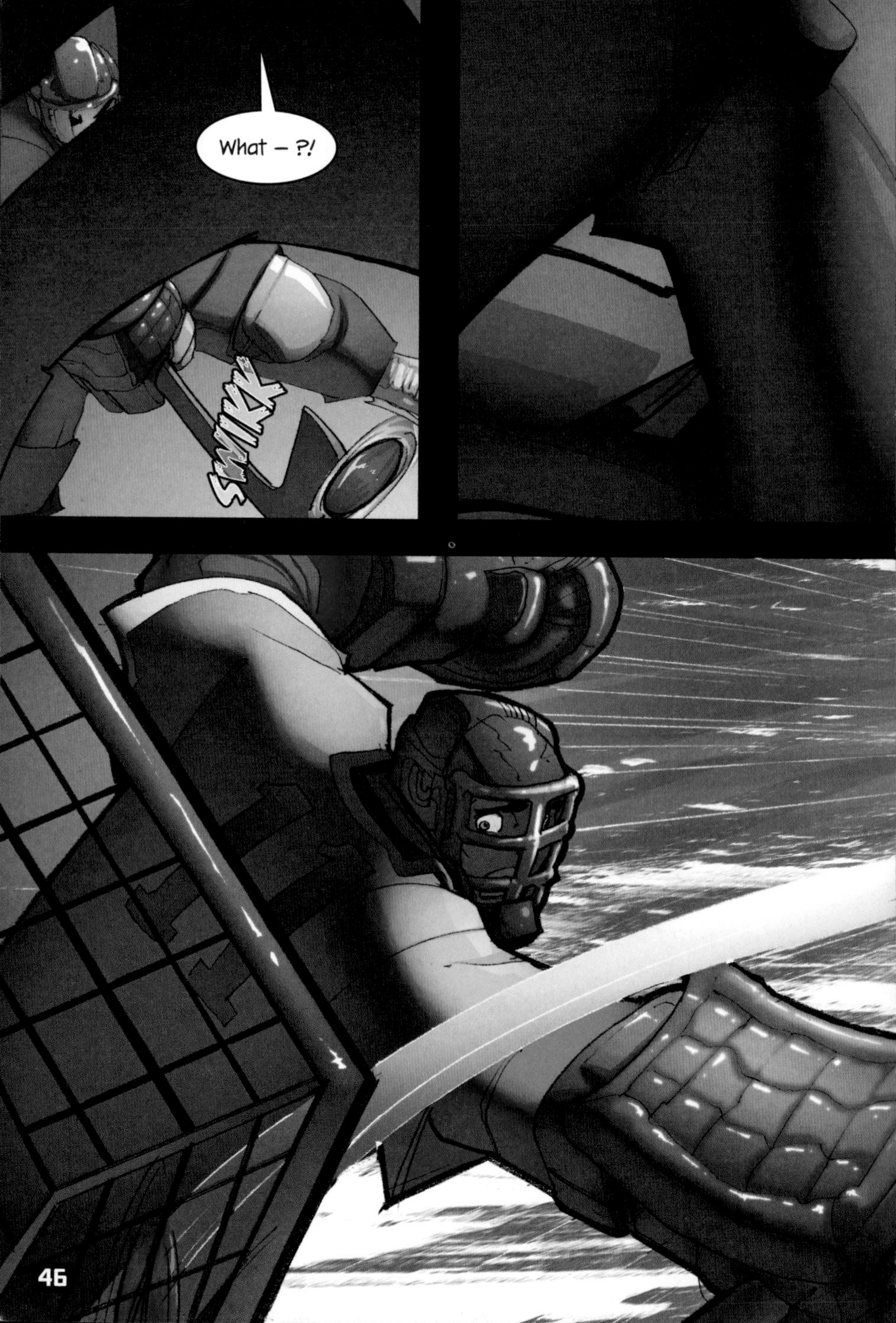
What – ?!
SWIKK

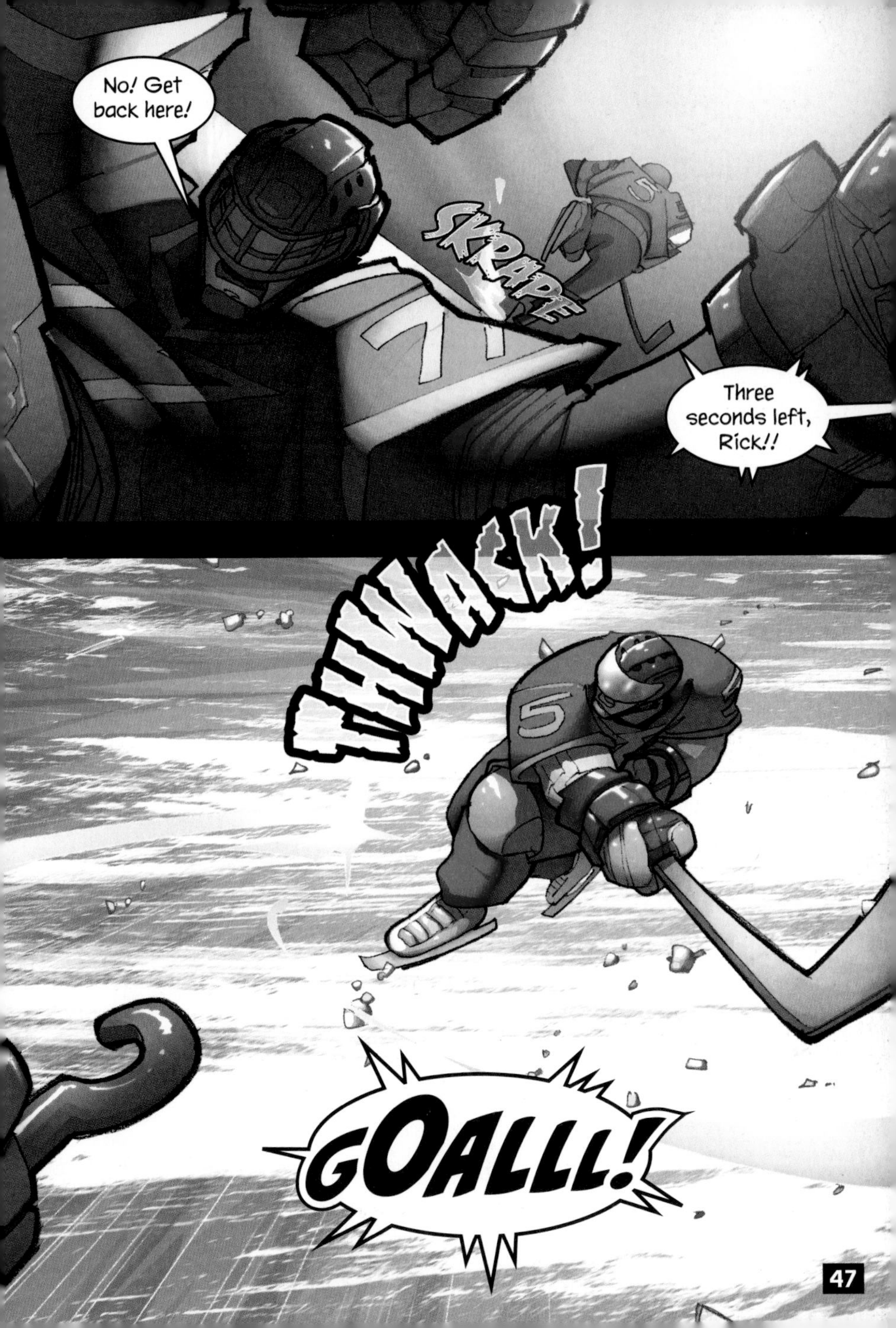
No! Get back here!
SKRAPE
Three seconds left, Rick!!
THWACK!
GOALLL!

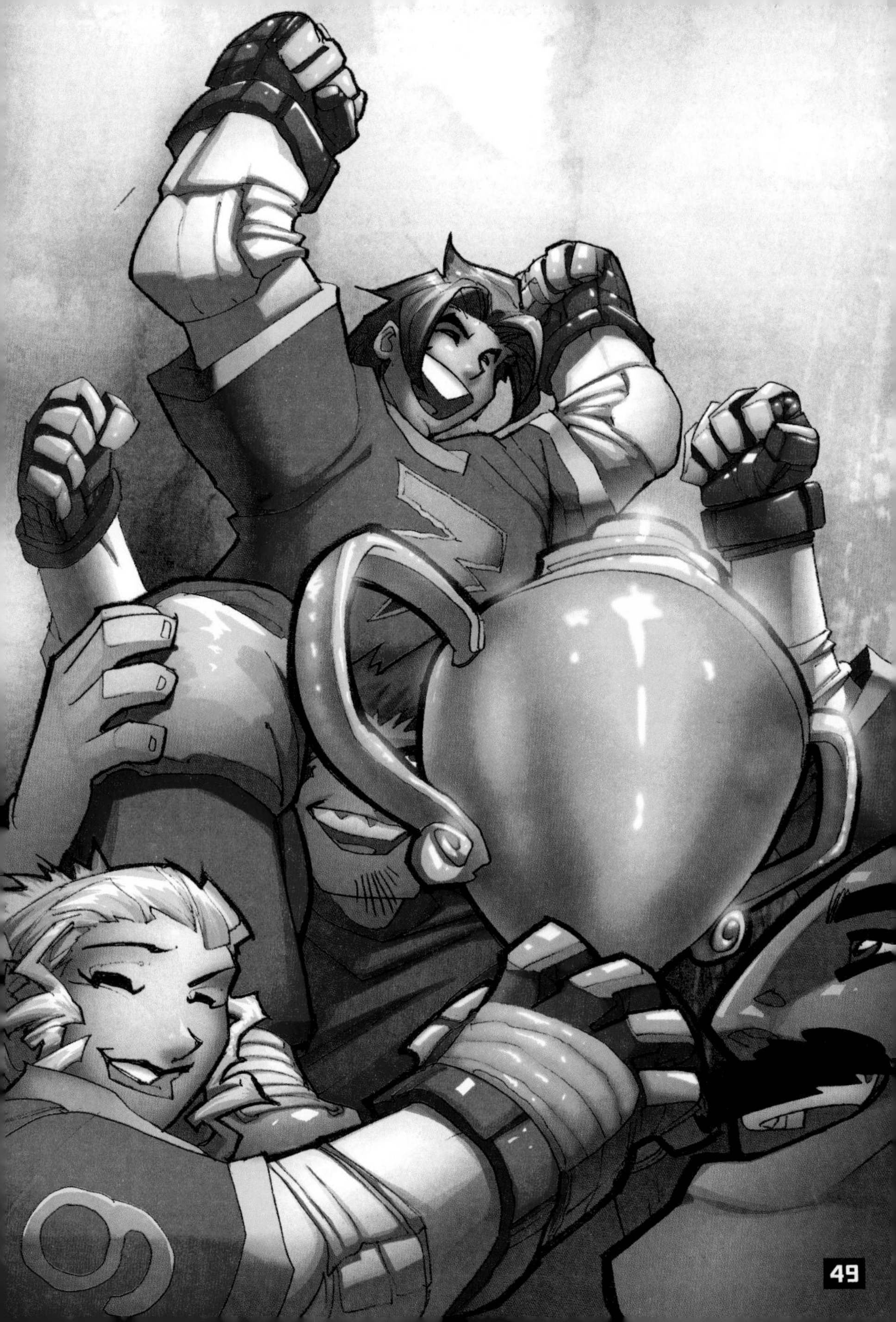

# SPORTS ZONE

## STGAME RECAP

KY

EY

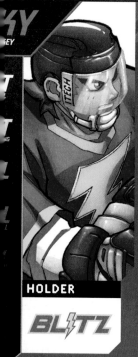

HOLDER

BLITZ

## RICKY'S REALITY CHECK EARNS HIM TEAM MVP — AND *THE STATE TITLE!*

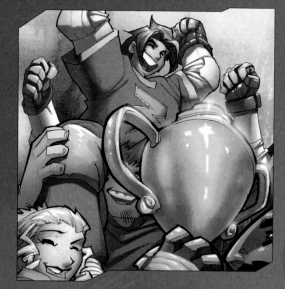

### Y THE UMBERS

*NAL SCORE:*
ITZ 4, RAPTORS 3

*ASON HIGHS:*
ALS: TAYLOR, 22
SISTS: HOLDER, 31
T TRICKS: JACOBS, 2

**STORY:**

In a shocking move, Coach Morelli moved the overly aggressive Holder from defenseman to right wing minutes before the big game. The risky switch paid off — Ricky was able to put his anger on ice, and went on to score the championship-winning goal. After the game, Ricky was named team MVP in a unanimous vote by his Blitz teammates.

Sports Illustrated KIDS

UP NEXT: SI KIDS INFO CENTER

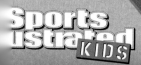

# SZ POSTGAME EXTRA

## WHERE *YOU* ANALYZE THE GAME!

Hockey fans were treated to an amazing game today when Ricky Holder and the Blitz ran right over the Raptors. Let's go into the stands and ask some fans for their perspectives on today's exciting championship game . . .

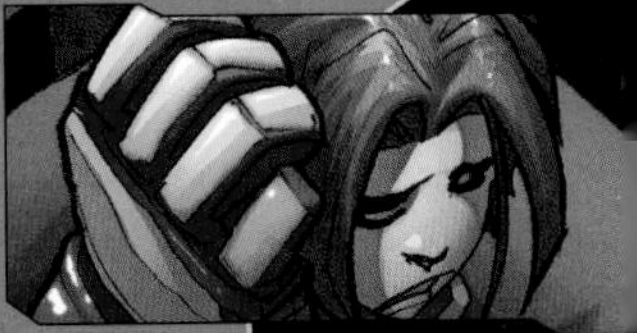

### DISCUSSION QUESTION 1

Ricky gets different advice from his friends and from his father. Who gives you better advice — your parents, or your friends? Why?

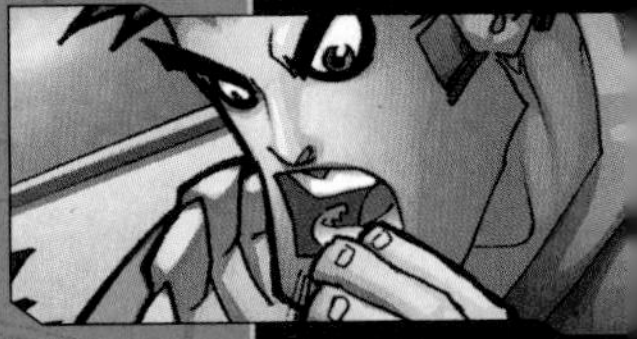

### DISCUSSION QUESTION 2

Mr. Holder puts a lot of pressure on his son, Ricky. How do you handle pressure? Can pressure ever be a good thing? Why or why not?

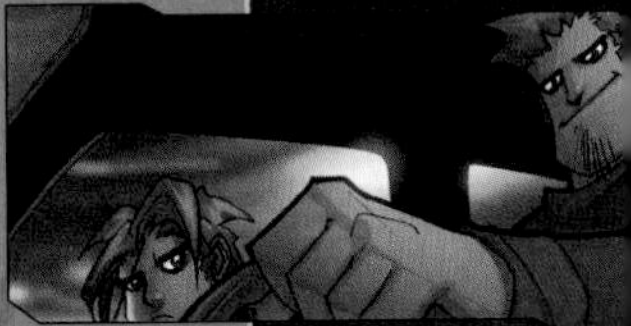

### WRITING PROMPT 1

Ricky feels trapped between his father's and his friends' expectations. Have you ever felt trapped? What was the situation? What did you do about it?

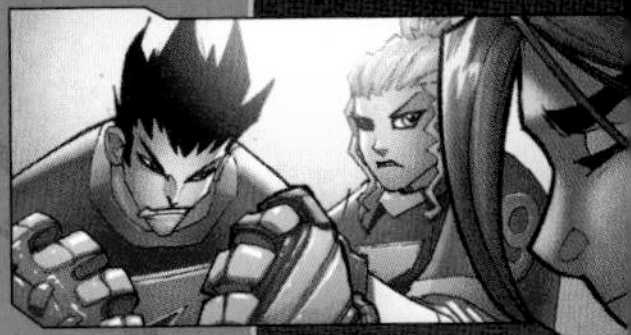

### WRITING PROMPT 2

Did Ricky's teammates handle his aggressive behavior the right way? What could they have done better? How can you help an angry friend?

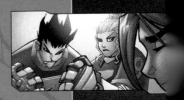

Sports Illustrated KIDS

# INFO CENTER

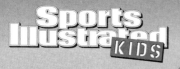

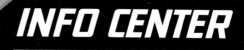

## GLOSSARY

**AGGRESSIVE** (uh-GRESS-iv)—making a forceful, total effort to win or succeed

**ASSIST** (uh-SISST)—the pass made to a scoring player just before a goal. A maximum of two assists can be given per goal.

**CHECK** (CHEK)—a hit made by a defending player against an opponent in an attempt to get the puck away from them or slow them down

**HIGH-STICKING** (HI-STIK-ing)—penalty called when a player's stick is raised above the waist when they contact another player

**INTENSITY** (in-TEN-suh-tee)—showing great energy, strength, or focus in a competition of some sort

**RESPONSIBLE** (ri-SPON-suh-buhl)—if you are responsible for something, then you caused it to happen

**SCRIMMAGE** (SKRIM-ij)—a game played for practice, usually with one team dividing its players into two opposing teams

**VOLUNTEERED** (vol-uhn-TEERD)—offered to do something, usually for no reward

# REATORS

## NEL YOMTOV › *Author*

The career path of Nel Yomtov has taken him from the halls of Marvel Comics, as an editor, writer, and colorist, to the world of toy development. He then became editorial and art director at a children's nonfiction book publisher. Now, Nel is a writer and editor of books, websites, and graphic novels for children. A harmonica-honking blues enthusiast, Nel lives in New York with his wife, Nancy. They have a son, Jess.

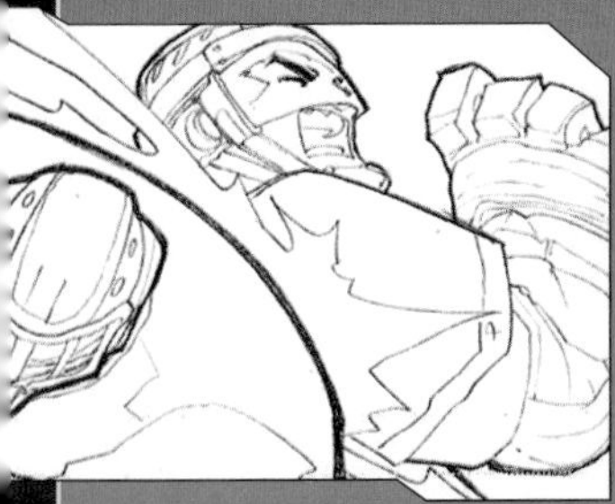

## GERARDO SANDOVAL › *Illustrator*

Gerardo Sandoval is a professional comic book illustrator from Mexico. He has worked on many well-known comics, including Tomb Raider books from Top Cow Production. He has also worked on designs for posters and card sets.

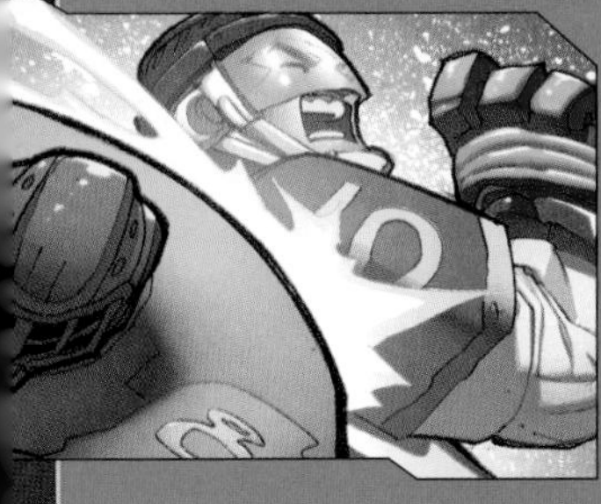

## BENNY FUENTES › *Colorist*

Benny Fuentes lives in Villahermosa, Tabasco in Mexico, where the temperature is just as hot as the sauce is. He works as a full-time colorist in the comic book industry for companies like Marvel, DC Comics, and Top Cow Productions. He shares his home with two crazy cats, Chelo and Kitty, who act like they own the place.

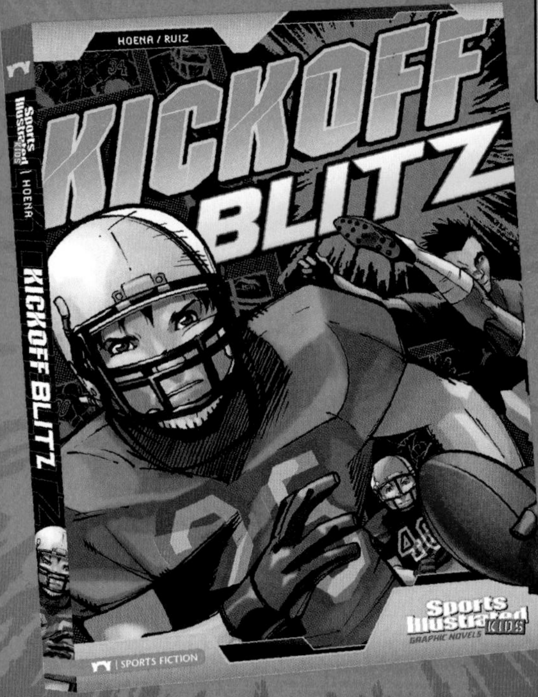

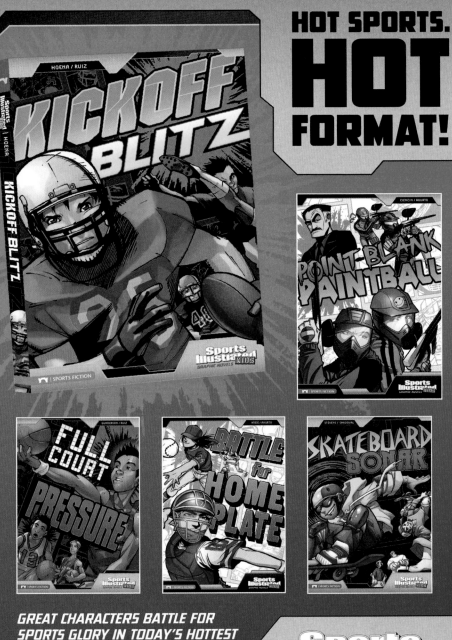

HOENA / RUIZ
KICKOFF BLITZ
Sports Illustrated KIDS GRAPHIC NOVELS
SPORTS FICTION
Sports Illustrated KIDS | HOENA
KICKOFF BLITZ


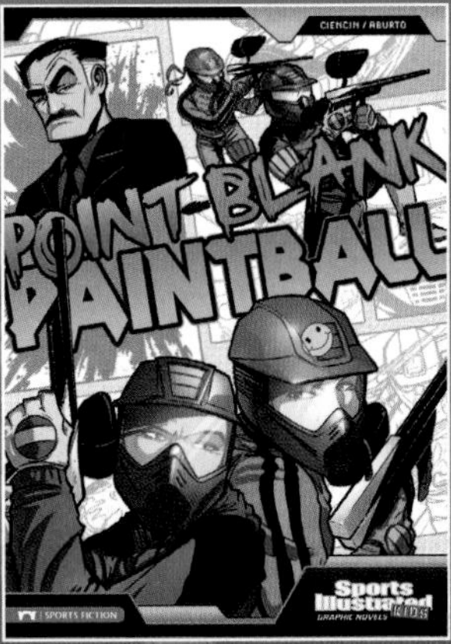

CIENCIN / ABURTO
POINT-BLANK PAINTBALL
SPORTS FICTION
Sports Illustrated KIDS GRAPHIC NOVELS


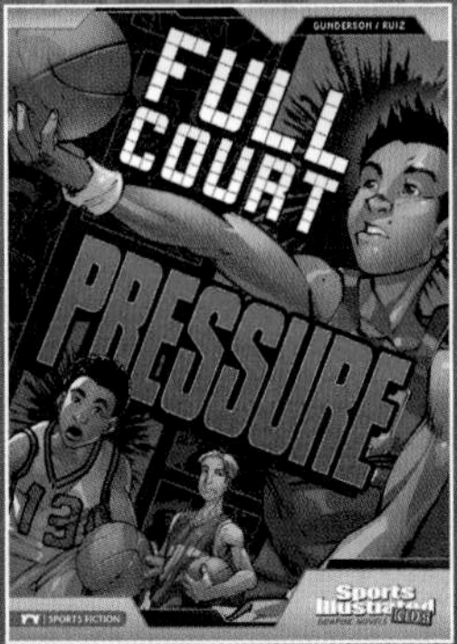

GUNDERSON / RUIZ
FULL COURT PRESSURE
SPORTS FICTION
Sports Illustrated KIDS GRAPHIC NOVELS


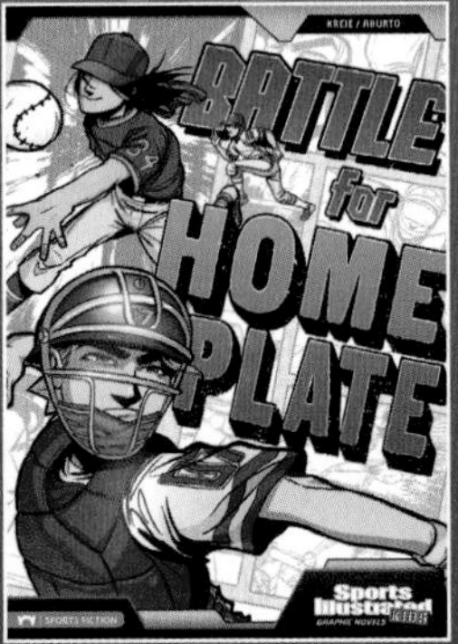

KREIE / ABURTO
BATTLE for HOME PLATE
SPORTS FICTION
Sports Illustrated KIDS GRAPHIC NOVELS


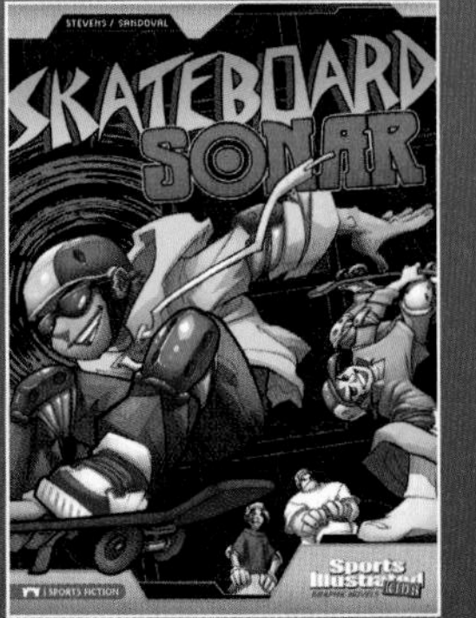

STEVENS / SANDOVAL
SKATEBOARD SONAR
SPORTS FICTION
Sports Illustrated KIDS GRAPHIC NOVELS

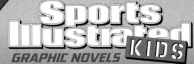

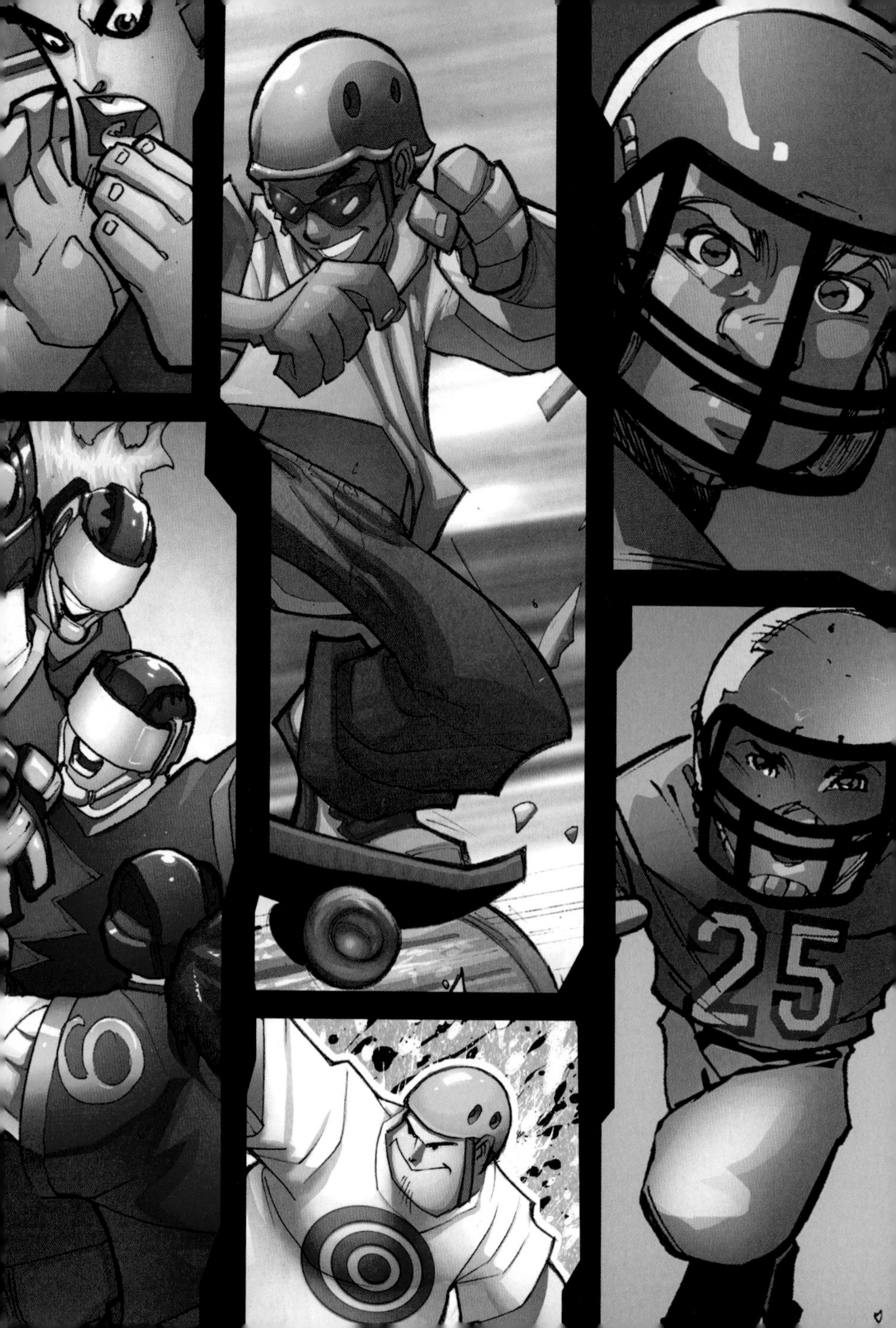
25

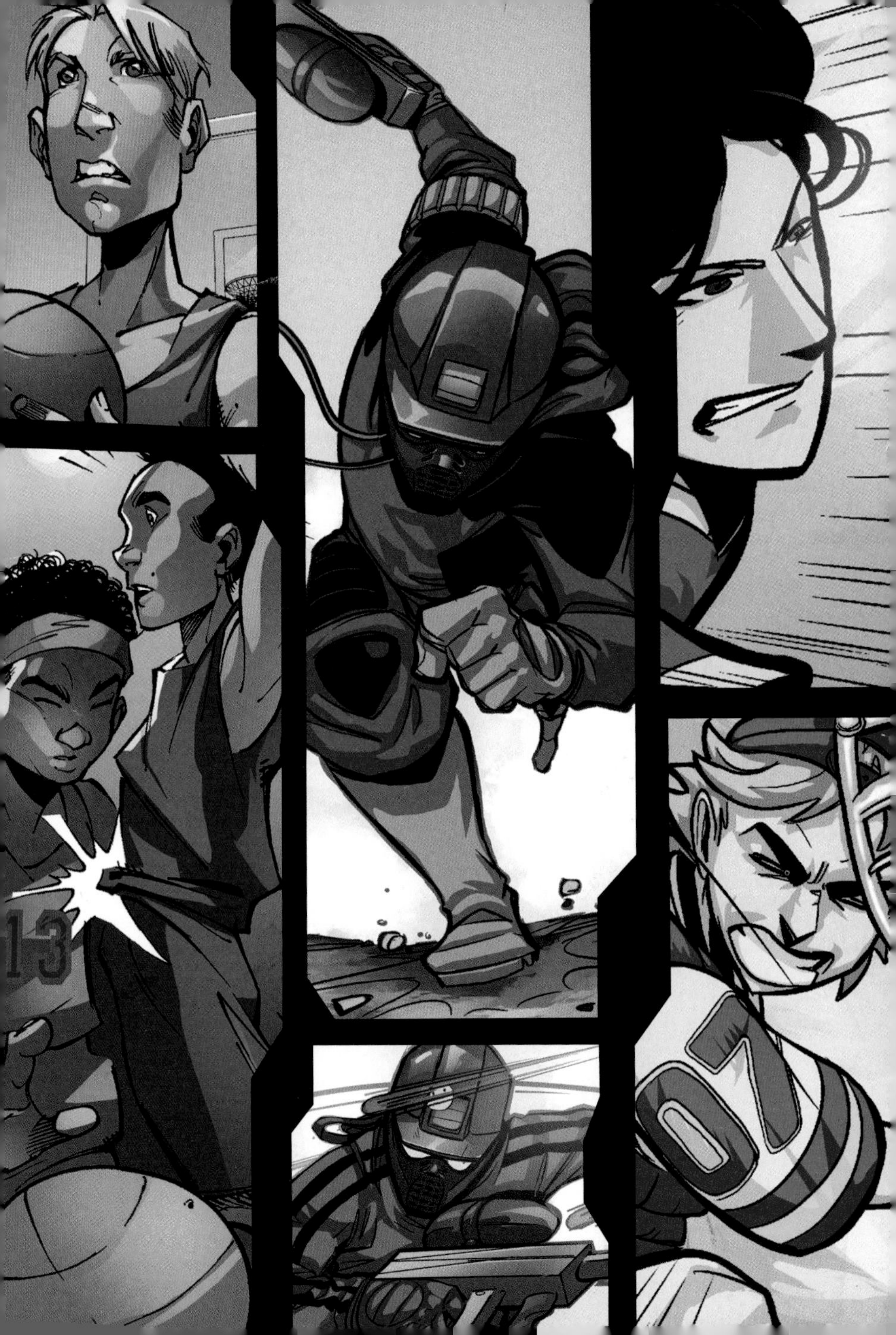

Sports Illustrated KIDS

GRAPHIC NOVELS

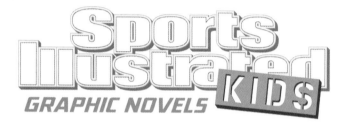

STONE ARCH BOOKS
a capstone imprint